THE TEN DAYS EXECUTIVE

SHORT STORIES

T0164038

ACKNOWLEDGEMENTS

Considering what a glorious procrastinator I am, I really have to thank the people that prompted me to action. To Barbara, Hannah and Jeremy who prodded and poked as gently and firmly as possible for this to get done; to my mother and father, Pearl and Claude, who always told me I could do and be whatever I wanted, and bought more books than perhaps their pockets could afford; Teressa, the most amazing sister ever; Charlie, who didn't mind when I left him to his own company while I wrote these stories; the MFA programme and UWI and the students in that programme who kept me on my toes creating dangerously; every writer who ever gave me honest feedback like Miss Erna and Miss Olive and Tanty Merle; my fairy godmother Rachel Manley who waved that wand and cracked that stick in turn; Funso Aiyejina for the patience, the edits, the support, the voice in my head; and Tony, who keeps believing even when I don't: Ase-Oh!

RHODA BHARATH

THE TEN DAYS EXECUTIVE

AND OTHER STORIES

PEEPAL TREE

First published in Great Britain in 2015
Peepal Tree Press Ltd
17 King's Avenue
Leeds LS6 1QS
England

ISBN13: 9781845232931

Supported using public funding by
ARTS COUNCIL
ENGLAND

CONTENTS

to
Karen Joanna and Poy Poy

Basil needed a work bad. It was almost eight months since he get lay off from the security job he had at the bus terminus.

"Patience, Basil, patience!" the manager, Mr. Iphil, had tried to reassure him.

"In a month time we go call you back. You know it had election. You know government change and they had was to shake up staff. Give we a few weeks. Once the dust settle we go hire back all we old workers."

Being a patient fella, Basil wait two months. He ain't bound to go back to work right away. In fact, the little layoff did really come like a holiday for him. At first he stay home and help Dulcie round the house and harass she a little bit, like any self-respecting husband. But then he start to feel tired hanging around the house and he went to see Mr. Iphil. Only to find out Mr. Iphil and all get fired and some new man name Beharry take he place and Beharry ain't have no time to see anybody and ain't know nothing about no job that some previous manager promise.

"Is a new dispensation now," Beharry say. "Check in the papers for when we have vacancies."

Is then Basil start to worry. He didn't figure that the change in government woulda affect him so. He realize that since he hair and Beharry hair wasn't the same texture, it probably mean that the two of them did vote for different parties and, as is a government job he was waiting on, he might have to wait a while. Maybe until the next elections if he party could get their act in order and get back in power.

Six more weeks pass and the little bit of money save up in the bank almost done and Dulcie starting to get vex because now Basil ain't have no money and he still want sex every day. Basil decide to try a little hustle. He borrow a partner car and pull bull with it in the night in areas where regular taxi wasn't working. It went okay for a while but it didn't last. The man want him to bring in sixty dollars a night and sometimes Basil was barely making that.

So, no sleep in the night and in the day he catching ass because Dulcie face swell up like crapaud after rain and she calling him good-for-nothing under she breath whole time. He getting real fed up and frustrated and sometimes when the frustration hit him so he feeling to cuff up she ass good and proper. But he fraid. She have a cousin who is a Special Branch police. A sweater police. Basil ain't fraid ordinary police but he don't make joke with sweater police. Anybody who could wear that kind of wool in this here heat have to be beast. He remember once when he was working as a security in a grocery he see two of them beat down a bandit. They start with him at the front of the grocery and end up in a storeroom in the back. The two of them take turns beating the man. After they finish subduing the suspect was straight hospital for him.

So Basil decide to leave Dulcie and she muttering alone, because he ain't want to get subdue. But still he studying day and night how to make money. He try wrapping grocery, but the pay real low. Four dollars an hour and he working from nine in the morning to all quality hour in the night. After one month, he leave that too. By then Dulcie stop muttering; she talking in plain English now.

"Basil, you real worthless for truth. My mother did warn me. She tell me you blight. But no, I hot, I want man. But like is a manicou I get and now look the pressure I seeing."

Basil remain quiet. He ain't say peep. He know the day he open he mouth, she go answer him back and he can't take it when woman answer him back. He know for sure for sure he go lash she. So to keep the peace, he hush he mouth.

By the time August month end reach, Basil was at the end of his rope. One night Dulcie outright blank him. She turn she back and steups.

"Why the ass you don't go and get a ten days," she ask him, "before you try to give me a nine months?"

The next day Basil went down by the Government Works office to see if he could get a ten days.

While he walking down Cemetery Street he remembering how he used to cut style on he partners when he see them working ten days. Men like Leonard and Frankie and Kyle. He remember how even when he was in school playing the fool he always used to say one thing he ain't doing is working ten days. He can't be so hard up he have to do manual labour. Nobody in he family ever line up to cutlass grass on the road or dig drain. All of them work for the government or in a bank; he ain't go be the first one to start.

But when he reach the government building, he almost turn back. Was like crazy ants on sweet bread. About a thousand people, some in line and all of them carrying on, some cussing hands down and demanding to see the foreman, because they cousin This or they uncle That tell them they getting a work this morning. Basil face fall one time; he get downpress. But when he study how sour Dulcie face go be when he reach home and tell she he ain't get nothing, he decide to try a thing. He decide to look for somebody in the line he know and see if he could kinda get a skip. He searching the faces and them but he ain't see nobody to spark off a talk with, no nice woman to give sweet eye and fall in step with. A Muslim fella lean up on a wall give him a half nod while he scanning. Basil stop.

"But wait nah," he say to heself. He shake he head, but he figure he go pursue it still.

"Darryl? Darryl from Government Sec? Boy, is long time. What vibes?"

"Salaam alaikum. Not Darryl no more boy. Is Malik now. I cool. What bout you? Seeing bout a little work and thing?"

Basil nod; taking him in and looking round him, he decide to jump in one time; small talk and catching up might cost him.

"Boy, I ain't know how to operate in this place, nah. How you does go about it?"

"Go by the foreman and let them write down your name. Then they does call you out for different gang and thing." Basil was immediately impressed by the amount of gold Malik wore in his mouth. One tooth even had a diamond stud.

"But it have people like ants here. I feel I mightn't get through and I have a wife home there. If she only hear I ain't get something is pressure. You ain't have a contact?"

Basil watch him and try out a smile after he say that because he know he ain't do it smooth enough. Malik shrug.

"Contact is a hard thing to make here. Men does take they time to decide who to make their friend. You know what I mean?"

Basil nod. Malik stand up straight. Basil stand up straight

too. Then some fellas approach them and start talking to Malik so Basil walk off.

Eventually he find he way to a table and give he name to a big woman with a red headtie who calling everybody "darling". She tell him stand up and wait. Basil see about three page of name in front of he own in the book. He heart sink.

He wait and wait; he name never call. But he noticing that plenty other fellas who was behind him in the line, some of them who was talking to Malik, get call and he start to wonder.

That evening, all he get from Dulcie was another long, wet steups.

"You ain't try hard enough, Basil. Goodnight."

The pressure was too much. He went on the block to look for Frankie and take a smoke. In a haze of ganja, the two of them start to plan Basil future.

"Boy, I telling you frankomen, the only way to get a work with URP now is to know somebody, get a Indian last name or turn Muslim. Even though you looking Creole, you have a little colour and your nose ain't spread like mine. Let we say your last name was Singh or Ramdath or something, you coulda get away with saying you is a dougla. Then you might have a chance. You have so much family, none of them in URP?"

Basil suck on the joint Frankie hand him.

"Boy, you ever hear bout a Huggins in URP? Huggins does only be bank manager and store manager, boy."

"Well, being as how all you so rich, it must have some Huggins in management who could find a job for you."

Basil ignore Frankie sarcasm.

"So since I ain't Indian and I ain't know nobody, no work?"

"Well, is either that or you have to turn Muslim, boy.

That is the only way I see you getting through. The Muslim and them does run everything in URP." Basil hand Frankie back the joint and cross he arms over he chest. For the next half hour, he hardly say a word. He thinking hard.

Dulcie was so damned vex over their money problems she wouldn't take on Basil. She mind hot with making ends meet and making sure the neighbours and them ain't find out she and Basil catching they ass to get by. But by the time she cool down she start to notice how he behaviour change up. She ain't know what to make of Basil. Whole time he moving quiet, quiet. He come home one morning with a book and whole day he lie down in the bedroom with it. All the steups she steups and quarrel she quarrel, pointing out that even though he ain't working it don't mean that it ain't have work round the house to do, Basil ain't say boo. He just reading.

That night she look for the book but she ain't find it. And when she come to bed well prepared to buff his ass for loafing whole day and then turn she back, he ain't even touch she. In fact, is he who turn he back. One time Dulcie get confuse. But she smart. She ain't let him know. She turn she back too and pull the sheet hard.

Next morning Basil get up, brush he teeth, drink a glass of water, tuck a parcel under he arm and leave the house. For three days, Dulcie ain't see him. By the time she vexation over and she start to worry, Basil walk back home cool cool. But he look different. He ain't shave the whole time he wasn't home.

The first thing to come in Dulcie head is that he have a next woman because Basil movements ain't making no sense. One minute he was all over she, the next minute he ain't taking she on and he moving funny. Disappearing for days at a time. She start to wonder who trying to mash up she living and take way she man. She start to ask round. When she bounce upon Frankie in the market one day she ask him point blank what going on with Basil.

"Like he have a woman or what? Is horn I getting horn?"

"Don't talk shit nah, woman," Frankie tell she. "Too besides, is more than a week now me self ain't see Basil. He riding partner these days is some fella name Malik."

"Ah worried," Dulcie confess. "When I do see him all he doing is lying down inside reading."

A whole month again pass. Nine months no work. Basil stop shaving, stop talking to Dulcie. Sometimes when she go in the room for something he bend down in a corner talking to heself and she can't make out nothing he saying.

"What happen? You working obeah or what?"

But Basil doing like he ain't hear. He ain't take she on. He get up, dust off and stretch out in the bed. The morning after that scene play off he went out. Dulcie start to brace she self for a next disappearance. Or worse than that. She telling sheself maybe she shouldn'ta ask him that question about obeah the night before. Maybe that little straw break the camel back.

"What I go do without Basil," she wonder. "He ain't working is true, but he ain't so bad as all that."

Dulcie study the man she was with before Basil. A fella name Cyril who used to beat she regular when he get frustrated or was out of work or both. She was with him for six years and in that time he make she throw away two children. Then she meet Basil and things change. The licks stop and Basil insist they go family planning. She wipe she eye.

Basil fed up, tell she she too quarrelsome. But she can't help but worry about their future. She study all the things she family say bout him and how she defend him and now it look like Basil was going to prove them right and she wrong. Basil was a good man, she know that; but if he didn't have a job, how other people would know that? If she didn't cuss him and light a fire under he ass, she wasn't sure he would try to find a job. Well, okay, yes he was trying. But she wanted him to try harder.

Dulcie wipe she face and let she mind drift a little.

"Maybe I was a little too quarrelsome," she tell she self. "Maybe I have to try to be a little sweeter. Maybe sweetness go do the trick."

That night, Dulcie lie down whole time listening to Basil breathe hard. She know he ain't sleeping because everytime she whisper he name or shift in the bed he stop breathing. As soon as the sun rise, she tell sheself she going put question to him. She watch he face next to she own; she could barely make him out with that beard. She wanted him to shave. She wanted him to talk to her again. She wanted the old Basil back.

He leave she in bed early that morning. She lie down under the sheet studying how to start. He come back and ask she for a scissors. She try to start but by the time she open she mouth he done find the scissors and gone.

"When he come out from the bathroom," she tell sheself. "I can't let him go out today with things sour between us so." When he come back in, Dulcie jump. All she could find to say was "Jeezanages!"

Basil leave the house with real pace that morning.

The crowd at the Government Works Office looked even larger that day. Christmas was two months away. If any of these fellas have woman like Dulcie, Basil thinking, they know they have to find some change to bring home. At least by the start of December.

His partner, Malik, was leaning up on the wall again.

"Asalaam alaikum, Malik," Basil greeted him.

Malik straightened up, "Alaikum salaam, Bro."

"The clothes fit you like is yours, brother."

Basil almost blush.

"I going to put down my name," he say, "I…"

"Relax, brother." Malik put up a hand to stop him. "I organize you already. All you have to do is wait."

When the foreman come out with the list, Basil try hard to hide he excitement. The whole crowd surge forward but he remain lean up on the wall next to Malik, cool as ice.

About fifty people get call and he ain't hear he name. He straighten up. Man from all side walking off and going in they gang while he, Basil, lean up on the URP Building wall like a jackass in the taj and tunic he borrow from he friend.

"Relax," Malik say, making a pumping downward motion with the palms of his hands. "I organize you." Basil studying what Dulcie go say if he come home without a work again. He know she go give him fatigue after how he carry on for the whole of the last month. Especially after this morning. "Relax?" Malik could relax. He coocoo done cook. He, Basil, ain't relaxing till he hear he name.

But the foreman reach the end of the list and Basil ain't hear he name. He ready to cry. He grit he teeth.

"Grin and bear it," he say, repeating a phrase he father used to use all the time when thing not going good. "Grin and bear it, Basil."

"…Malik Mohammed, Faraz Mohammed," the foreman reading. Was the charge-hand list he calling out now. Basil make ready to leave, a heaviness in he stomach. He wondering how he go face Dulcie.

"Khalid Ali, Yasin Abdul, George Peters, Mustapha Hussain…"

Basil jump. Yasin Abdul? He say Yasin Abdul? A charge

hand? Allah-u-akbar! God really great in truth! He look at Malik. He partner smiling at him all over he face. Basil feel like he coulda kiss him.

He couldn't wait to see the sourness leave Dulcie face when she get the news. He, Basil Huggins, alias Yasin Abdul, was now part of the management team. Allah-u-akbar.

Sempo led Teresa to the Nissan Bluebird, his heart beating fast fast. He was trying hard to appear laid back but his head was spinning. Today, he'd talk to Miss Angelina about her daughter. With luck, everything could be arranged when he was at her house.

As he slipped into the driver's seat he asked her if she wanted something to drink, then cursed himself for making a false move; it wasn't normal for taxi drivers to offer their passengers drinks. He saw his thoughts mirrored in Teresa's eyes and the hint of a smile flashing across her face. He had to play his hand carefully with this one.

"No thanks," she said almost inaudibly. "I good."

She seemed relaxed and at ease, even a little bored.

He stole a glance at his own clothes, the light blue short-sleeved shirt neatly tucked into shiny black trousers, only slightly scuffed black patent leather shoes and navy-blue socks – suddenly too blue for his liking. He didn't have to look like Cary Grant or Rock Hudson, but it wouldn't have hurt to be wearing black socks. Silk, if possible, like the ones he'd seen advertised in the shop window at Bachu's. Not that she would have noticed. She was staring straight ahead, as if seeing the road for the first time. He caught a glimpse of himself in the rear-view mirror and only just resisted the urge to run his hand through his tousled hair. She might think him vain, or, at least, nervous.

"You will have to direct me, eh," he said, to keep a conversation going, "I ain't really sure where you living."

She nodded but said nothing.

"Is near the ice factory, right?"

Another nod. He'd have to kick-start the conversation or they'd be pulling up in front her house before they'd exchanged a dozen words. This wasn't going too smooth at all. By now she should have been flirting with him…

His mind went back to the first time he'd seen her. He was leaning against the grey Bluebird when she appeared out of nowhere, crossed the main road and got into a taxi. She had jet-black curly hair and her skin was so fair it was pink, like she was Spanish or Portuguese. She looked like she might be a secretary or shop girl, something upscale. Right away he knew he wanted to find out who she was. On that first day he'd whistled softly, nudged his friend Harry and motioned in her direction with his chin. Harry had taken one brief look, sized her up as out of their league, and gone right back to hustling passengers with Spanish, Lochan, Randy and the others.

But Sempo had been intrigued. The image of the hem of her flowered dress swinging gaily as she bent down to get into the old Falcon had remained with him until he saw her again a few weeks later. She was standing under the awning of the Bank of Nova Scotia, waiting for a taxi, trying to avoid the blistering sun. Sempo pretended to be busy hustling passengers for a Curepe trip, but he hardly took his eyes off her. He was not sure she knew she was being watched, though once or twice he got the impression she was watching him out of the corner of her eye.

Was she waiting for somebody, he'd wondered. Maybe

Miss Prim and Proper not as innocent as she look. Maybe is a man friend she waiting for…

"What the hell? Who driving this car?" Randy's voice had broken into his thoughts. "Aye, Semps, you eh working today or what? Yuh full! Either peel out or let somebody take your five and go!"

For a moment, Sempo was tempted to tell Randy to take the frigging five and go. But, whoever it was might be late. It might take half an hour or something for she man to come.

"Alright! Alright! I out of here."

With a long, bold look in the direction of the green dress, he hopped into his car, hit the key, threw it into first gear and pulled out into the traffic. Feeling the urge to hear some music, he reached down and put the radio on.

"…Can't hurry love./Oh, you just have to wait./She said love don't come easy/It's a game of give and take./ How much more…"

He changed the station. Later for Diana Ross and the Supremes. Now was not the time for all this heartbreak, tabanca music. He wanted to hear something to take his mind off the girl. Not moon over her like a lovesick fool.

"…So ah want yuh to write all yuh family name/ On ah piece of paper fuh me…"

There was a buzz of approval in the taxi.

"We go take the kaiso, Drive," the passenger seated behind him said.

Sempo put both hands on the wheel and let Zandolee entertain the taxi for the remaining minutes of the song.

But then all the way to Curepe, he could not get rid of the phrase that had leapt into his mind: "Zandolee", it ran, "…find yuh hole! Find yuh hole, zandolee!" And on the way back from Curepe he was thinking about what he would do the next time he saw her. After all, he chuckled to himself, you could make track for 'gouti to run on, but lappe does make he own way. And he was not no 'gouti; he was a lappe!

On Wednesday afternoon he'd seen her for the third time. She was alone again, on this occasion dressed in red. She was carrying a blue house-and-land umbrella; she obviously didn't enjoy the broiling afternoon sun.

Fortunately for Sempo, things were slow on the stand; there were plenty of cars with only a dribble of passengers. He ran back to the Bluebird and took it around the corner. Then, checking the red dress was still in front of Nova Scotia, he hustled over to the Chinese parlour to buy two soft drinks. He walked slowly towards her with the icy-cold Solo Apple J bottles dripping cold water all over his hands.

"Miss, I see you looking a little thirsty standing up here in the hot sun," he said, "so, I bring this for you." He produced the bottle with a flourish, aware that half the taxi stand must be watching how the scene playing out. If he had to take any talk later, he at least wanted them to acknowledge his flair.

She let her gaze wander slowly down from his head to his feet. Then, she raised a palm in a gesture of refusal and turned her back on him, so she was almost facing the reflective glass of the bank's window.

He stood there like a statue, left hand stuck out towards her, one bottle of Apple J tightly clasped between his fingers, his right hand holding the other bottle limply at his side, an embarrassed smile frozen on his lips.

She fingered the strap of her black handbag, folded her arms over her bosom and seemed to study her reflection in the window.

From across the street, the hecklers set off like fireworks.

"Boy, Semp, red woman is trouble, boy, big trouble. And when they high red like that one… Worse!" Randy's comment brought an explosion of laughter from the crowd of taxi-drivers.

"Watch yourself, boy! You playing with fire."

Sempo ignored them. He was looking at her reflection and thought he saw laughter in her eyes and the beginnings of a smile at the corner of her mouth. Shifting the weight from his left leg to his right, he decided to use her amusement at his embarrassment to his advantage.

"I buy this for you. No strings…"

She cut him short.

"Look, Sir, I don't mean to be rude but I don't talk to strange men or accept gifts from them. So, thanks, but, no thanks."

Sempo was suddenly very conscious of the heat of the sun beating down on him. He held his pose while behind him his comrades continued to cheer. Slowly, theatrically, he dropped his left hand back to his side. That "Sir" was a razor on his jugular, a tree across his highway, a red light at his intersection, a zwill on the thread of his mad bull. She was playing hard to get; he would have to give her time.

He'd been sure he would see her again, so he snapped the cap off his drink with his teeth and took a long swig. Then, he turned smartly on his heels and went back to his car, a carefree smile locked on his face.

By the time he had resumed hustling passengers at the Curepe queue, she had crossed the street and got into her regular Longdenville taxi.

The fatigue from his fellow drivers soon began.

"Ou ka pis plu ho pasé tjou'w," Spanish, the driver of the Super Saloon, the flashiest car on the beat, told him.

"You biting off more than you could chew, boy," Harry

21

concurred, "Never piss higher than yourself, it go fall in your face. That girl go only get you in trouble. Forget about she."

Sempo was not so easily put off.

"All you know she?" he asked.

"Yeah. She name Teresa. She father is one of the main goldsmith in Chaguanas,.." Harry said.

"Yes, Maharaj," Spanish added. "She mother is a Portuguese. The mother father was a jeweller. He had an apprentice in he shop. A little Indian fella who take up the trade, and take up the man daughter too. The daughter had was to leave home. They set up their own establishment on a side street in Chaguanas, until they get popular enough to move to the Main Road."

Sempo nodded. He liked stories of people fighting odds and triumphing. Hadn't he escaped the backwaters of South Trinidad to become a successful taxi driver, plying his trade in all these mysterious places, like Marabella, Couva and Pt Lisas, he had only heard about as a boy?

"Boy," Harry warned, "that family ain't easy you know." Sempo nodded but, this time, he was no longer listening. His mind was made up.

His interest grew into an obsession. He would ask everyone, even his passengers, about Teresa's family, and soon he was able to piece together the rest of her story.

Apparently, at the behest of his Catholic wife-to-be, Teresa's father, had abandoned his faith and the couple had eloped and got married at in a civil ceremony at the Red House. A year later, to ease Angelina's conscience about not having made vows before God, a quiet church ceremony was conducted by an accommodating priest. Though that was the last time Mukesh set foot in a church, he celebrated Christmas and Easter with all the gusto of a born Christian.

The story intoxicated Sempo. Teresa's father had made

changes for love, and Teresa's mother was a woman after his own heart; he understood her. He wanted to share his story of escape with her, to tell her how he too had faced oppression. The ninth of eleven children growing up in a wooden hut in the back of nowhere in South Trinidad, his only choices in life had been subsistence farming on the family's plot of land, or trying his hand at some sort of trade. He wanted neither. Toiling at the hard earth in Lengua at the mercy of sun and rain was not for him, and there was no trade he seemed good at. Masonry and carpentry did not come easily to him, and he did not have the money to acquire the tools to be a welder or mechanic.

But he had one real skill: cards. Nobody he knew could read a deck, or an opponent's face, better than he. Nobody had a better poker face, even in the face of disaster.

Whenever there were All Fours competitions, Sempo was there, usually paired with a partner who was willing to let himself be led. But the pots, already small, had to be shared, and more and more he felt it was not worth his while. He switched to whappie. That was when he started to win big. And lose too. But he won more often than he lost, and one day, Sempo won an old Datsun 120Y from a foolhardy gambler who'd reached the bottom of his pockets.

The car had given him the start he needed. He began pulling bull from Lengua to San Fernando, four passengers at a time, five when he could squeeze them in, until he had enough saved for the Bluebird. He had been the proud owner of the new car for just two days when he left Lengua. That was seven years ago. He never went back. And now, here he was, ready to make another of those huge leaps in a life by making Teresa his wife.

She, too, would be his luck. Who knows? Maybe he could eventually buy another car, and become a fleet owner instead of just a driver. A real taxi service. He would call it Sempo and Sons. They would have a sign, call cards. He would have a phone! And an office to run the business from. Maybe right on the Chaguanas Main Road self. It sounded nice, real nice. Just thinking about it gave him a warm feeling. It felt good too to think about Teresa having his children, four or five little half-Portuguese, half-Indian beti and beta, eating sada roti and baigan and raising Cain and Abel.

But with me in the mix, he laughed softly to himself, they go be more than half Indian.

"And if I could talk to she mother about she," he mused, "that go be more than half the battle."

His chance had come sooner than he expected. The car in which Teresa usually went home was having gearbox trouble and the owner, Lochan, came looking for someone to take her home in his stead. The fellas on the stand, ready for a laugh, immediately volunteered Sempo. The Longdenville-Chaguanas route was out of the way and less profitable than Chaguanas-Curepe, because there was no guarantee of a full return trip.

Sempo never hesitated.

"All right, Uncle, I go carry she. But is only as I know you long time I doing this favour, eh."

"…You have to direct me, eh. I ain't really too sure where you living."

She nodded assent.

"Is near the ice factory, right?"

More nodded agreement.

"How far from it?" Let me see you nod for that one, he said to himself.

"Well, it's approximately half a mile, something like that. On the same side of the road."

Sempo couldn't get past her use of "approximately". He rolled it over in his mouth, barely stopping himself from saying it aloud. She would deal with the customers of the taxi service and say words like approximately to them when they called for their cars.

He looked at her out of the corner of his eye. She looked good in the front seat of the car beside him. She belonged in the Bluebird. He could see that, but could *she* see it. Would Miss Angelina and Mr. Mukesh be able to see it.

He felt sure he could impress her parents with how hardworking and knowledgeable he was.

He would tell them he had driven passengers to Port of Spain many times and spent time in the city. They would appreciate that he was a well-travelled man with a world view, something not too many taxi-drivers had. Harry, Randy, Spanish and the others were generally content with the Chaguanas-Curepe route, and he would often tell them that they needed to get out into the world the way he had. True, Chaguanas-Curepe yielded a good day's earnings and sometimes even Sempo was content with that. But there were times when he hungered for the bustle of the capital and all the important activities that took place there. When he spoke to Teresa's parents, he would be sure to casually mention Salvatori Building and the Red House and Frederick Street and the Savannah, so as to let them know that he was a man who really knew his way around.

Sempo was still engrossed in his private thoughts (and his passenger in hers) when he realised that they were entering Longdenville. He was running out of time and had yet to make his play. In a moment, they were passing the ice factory. Before he knew it, she was pointing down the road to a red, wrought-iron gate and instructing him to "Stop there".

She didn't get out immediately, as he had expected. She sat, as if waiting for something. Sempo realised he had prepared nothing to say to her. He tried to smile, but found he couldn't.

"Well," she said after a while, "I'm home."

And with a quick fixing of skirt, manoeuvring of legs, and opening of the door, she disappeared behind a creaking gate.

His chance had come and gone. He was left with all the fine words and jokes he had strung together to impress Miss Angelina and Mr. Mukesh.

From somewhere behind the gate, he heard a woman's voice ask, "Teresa, is that you?" followed by Teresa's dutiful, "Yes, Ma."

He got out from behind the wheel and looked up at the house. There were four huge windows at the front, all decorated with blue-slate quarry stones. Along one side he counted more eight windows. The terrace was cordoned off by intricate wrought-iron work and ran along the front and down one side of the house.

The place was immense in comparison to his two-bedroom bachelor affair in Chaguanas, not to mention the hut he had left behind in Lengua. Downstairs was the business place – where the jewellery was made – and upstairs the dwelling house.

Along the terrace, on the upper level, he caught a glimpse of a tall, fair, older version of Teresa. Miss Angelina. Was she looking at him, studying him, sizing him up?

Sempo looked at himself. The patent leather shoes looked like a cheap Bata number, and the blue socks as out of place on his bony shins as a cassocked priest at a chutney fete. It was obvious that he'd ironed his trousers himself instead of sending them to the Chinese laundry as he did with his Sunday-best clothes. His rumpled shirt looked threadbare. He felt every inch a coolie from deep south.

Through the metal gate, a man sitting on a low bench was peering at him, a squat middle-aged man wearing a stained merino and a pair of dingy khaki trousers rolled up around his ankles.

"Afternoon, boy. What you waiting for? What you want?" The man paused to look at Sempo with a questioning look.

"Lochan ain't pay you? You want money? You want me to go get the boss?"

He reminded Sempo of an uncle, the one everyone said he resembled.

Sempo suddenly felt foolish. Lochan had paid him. So why was he standing there in front of the people's house, hoping to find some way to make it with these rich people's daughter? He was out of his mind. Stark, staring mad.

His shoulders sagged. He climbed in behind the wheel of the Bluebird, put the car in first gear, eased off the clutch and with one last wistful look at the Maharaj mansion inched his way down the street, imagining the strains of "Here Comes the Bride" in the steady drone of the motor.

BEFORE I DEAD

This morning I carry a gun because they get me vex. Usually I does have a knife on me; it have something about the way it does feel: solid and safe like when you swimming in the river or the sea, and even though the water deep or rough, once you stretch out your foot you go feel the seabed underneath you and know you safe. It have fellas in my school that does tote gun, but I never really feel that is for me. Gun like it have it own mind, like once it in your hand you can't control it. Where I living in Arouca, I see men dead from own-way gun. The gun just reach in man hands and next thing you know it shoot off and is dead a man dead and the fella with the gun ain't even sure how he kill the man and if is really he that kill the man.

It have plenty chance to get gun. You just have to stand up on the junction long enough and think about a gun and a man go walk up to you and offer you one. You could even rent one if you can't afford to buy it. Fellas does rent gun and bring it in school to show off. All recess and lunch time they in a corner in the classroom, pulling it out, stroking it, pointing it. Whenever they point it, fellas does scatter, they ain't stupid. And if you see them with gun in they hand. They does have this kinda half smile, that is not really a smile, is really a "what if" expression. Like, "What if I pull this trigger, boy?" or, "What if I ride shots for that fella in

Arima who disrespect me and my girl by the Velodrome the other night. I go show him. I go show him…"

Other fellas does want to hold the gun but they don't let them unless them is a good good partner, because they could never really tell if a fella holding a secret grudge against them and waiting to fire off the gun at them. Most times is only one bullet in the gun because to buy bullets expensive, so they does buy one for protection, but really the protection is having the gun in they hand and pretending that the chamber might be full. Although fellas know is bluff they bluffing, since they ain't know which chamber have the bullet, they will go along with the bluff and respect the gun.

With a knife now, is you they does respect, because knife is skill. You could stab a man and make as little damage as a scratch or you could kill him. It depend on if you know how to use it. With a knife you could feel yourself slicing through flesh; you can't feel that with a bullet. Guns good to kill fellas you ain't really know or care about; but a knife is for more personal things. If a fella take your girl, you have to get him with a knife. Wait for a fete or something, get your partners and them and ride for him, and in the thick of the bacchanal stick him with the knife, twist it in he guts, feel he flesh moving aside to make way for the metal. You watch him in he eye so he know who doing it and why you doing it. If he have a gun, though, it really ain't matter how much skill you have.

Is one of the security guard on the compound that get me vex. Ah mean, I don't trouble nobody and I was going about my business cool, cool. It have plenty thing people could say about me, eh. They could say I does smoke weed and they could say I does cuss stink when I vex. But they can't say I does trouble people. Since I is a little fella I prefer to keep myself to myself and leave people alone. Everybody know that.

So when just so one of them security walk up to me and say, "I hear you was interfering with a girl," I get vex. One thing I don't like is for people to say I do thing I never do. I, Saleem Mustapha, is one man who go never put Allah out of he thoughts and harass a girl just so. And is the kind of girl too! Shelly Ann? It ain't have nothing special about Shelly Ann! She force-ripe like all them other Compre girls. Same powder on she neck, same fancy hairdo, although she ain't going nowhere, same loud voice and cussing people if they watch she too hard. The fellas does call she Clothes Clip Shelly Ann. Squeeze she head and she foot open. So how this guard could think that Shelly Ann could be special enough for me to trouble she?

And was the guard attitude too! They does move like everybody is prisoner in this place. They does walk up to you and get on as if them own you, as if them and the law is the same thing. So they grab you by your shirt and drag you in a corner, embarrassing you in front of all your friend and them, asking you all kind of question fast fast so you can't answer, and then, although they pull you in a corner, they talking hard hard for everybody to hear.

"You name Saleem, right?"

Mostly people does call me by my nickname, Taj, so when I hear Saleem I know is office business. One minute I strolling down the courtyard good, good, next minute I jam up in a corner next to the janitor room. Everybody on the corridor watching and I seeing people slow down to take in the scenes just in case it have any action.

"Is you name Saleem, right?" they ask me again. I nod. I sizing them up, because me ain't really fraid none of them. Them ain't no law, them ain't no police. Them is just security and I will tell them they ain't have no jurisdiction over me. If they want to question me they have to carry me by Mr. Pollard office. They could try all the scare tactics they want, they ain't getting me to talk about nothing. I done tell them who I is. Now is up to them to do something.

"What you want to know my name for?" I ask the guard straight in he face. The jackass hold my shirt collar tighter, like he feel that go frighten me. Man, I watch him right in he eye and steups. I have time. We could stand up in the corridor whole day for all I care.

By this time, big crowd and thing looking on. I getting more vex because one thing I don't like is embarrassment. Fellas want to know what happening and the girls and them only giggling and pointing at me. I feeling the comfort of the knife strap on to my leg and I feel better even though I know I can't use it. I see my partner Tush in front of the crowd.

"Don't dig nothing, Taj, boy," he shout out and I know he do that just to vex them. "I have your back, my boy. Dem MTS can't do nothing outta the way." I give him a nod. Tush like to harass men, but he and me real tight. I know he have my back and he go check on me to see what going down. Them MTS security does be liming round the Block in twos all the time, waiting to catch one of we with weed or cigarette or girl. The two that hold me, De Freitas and Singh, like to harass the students. If you only come in the schoolyard with your little half-pack of Benson and Hedges to sell, they taking it away and whole week they searching you to see what they find. If they in a bad mood, they sending you to the office and telling the principal they smell weed on you.

De Freitas is a red fella from Grande who feel because he big and strapping he is a big sawatee, but me ain't fraid he. Is the Indian, Singh, who is the trouble man. Singh does wear black gloves on he hand and he ain't have no problem with a little violence. "Is for a worthy cause," I hear him say once. He does move up easy, easy on men, as if he just going to ask them a question and then he does squeeze they balls hard hard so they can't answer because the pain too much. It have fellas say he does tote a piece, because he is a precepted officer. I never see the gun but other fellas say they see him with it under he clothes. I ain't putting it past him.

Anyway, since Singh and them can't use gun on the school compound, they does substitute the plastic baton in their waist. Is to see them drawing this baton when they catch one of we. Singh have a way he does wring up your shirt so you almost standing up on your toes and then he does put the baton between your legs sometimes and ram it up hard and crush your balls. I see real men cry when he do that. The first time he catch me for some stupidness he ask me my name and I, playing smart, tell him, "Assalaam alaikum." Since then he does always mock me, although he find out my real name. "Sallymally koom is your name, boy?" Or, he go tell he partner, "Eh eh, look Sallymally Koom passing."

He does mainly target the niggers on the compound. Sometimes dry, dry, he go call a boy in the corridor and start to search him. It had one time Tush and me was walking down the corridor in Block C and he call out, "Aye, nigger boy, drift and come over here." Boy, Tush ain't miss a beat. One time he answer back, "Yes, Daddy, I comin now." Tush get he balls squeeze that day but he ain't cry. We laugh we belly full because Singh done dark he dark, and when Tush give him that answer he face turn black like coal.

So anyway, yesterday, one minute they questioning me in the corridor, next minute is walk they walking me to the office. Singh hand still tight on my arm. I see Shelly Ann sitting down on a chair waiting and I watch she hard. I want to ask she what going on, but I cool myself. Singh and he partner waiting. I waiting too. After a while, Mr. Pollard come out of the principal office and call we. Shelly Ann get up and Singh let me go and I follow she and both of we sit down in the office. But the Principal ain't sit down; he sorting papers and adjusting he glasses. That is one thing does get me vex about Mr. Pollard, he and his damn glasses. He done short and softy-softy looking and then on top of that he insist on wearing these glasses with thick thick lens, and he always playing with them.

"So, Saleem, I hear you're in trouble again?"

"Sir, I don't know nothing about no trouble, sir." I leave it there. Let he come out and tell me what they have me here for. All this time Shelly Ann sit down cool cool; she ain't say a word. I watching she out of the corner of my eye, trying to figure she out. But she watching straight ahead so I feel I have to wait for Mr. Pollard to clear things up.

"Miss Williams says you interfered with her. Is that so?" I know I was looking confuse. I coulda almost see how I was looking, sit down there mouth open and close, open and close like a fish in a net.

"Interfere with Shelly Ann?" Pollard have to be joking! Shelly Ann? Clothes-Clip Shelly Ann? The same Shelly Ann who get parry when she was in Junior Sec? The same Shelly Ann who does be taking man down by the Agri-Science building every week? The same Shelly Ann who sitting down there and can't watch me in my eye? Me interfere with she? Everybody interfere with she. But never me! I ain't have time for rat!

Well, I get blue vex. Is this shit they pull me down in the office for? Since when anybody does believe anything she say? They have to come better than that! I know Mr. Pollard expecting me to protest and say, "No, sir, not me, sir." But I smarter than he. More in that mortar than this Shelly Ann pestle.

"All yuh have a witness, Sir?" I ask.

"Yes," he say and the word come out like a sigh because same time he say it he breathe out.

"Who is the witness?"

Mr. Pollard watch me like if he sorry for me. He take a long tired breath. "Jason Callender said he saw you pulling at Miss Williams' clothes in Room 40."

Oh-ho, so that is it. From the time I hear Jason Callender I done cipher out what going on. No maths in that. I know real fellas who is imps, but Callender have to be the biggest imps I know. You know the joke about how when you born the doctor slap your head and not your bottom? Well, with Callender that really happen. He is one of them that can't afford to buy cigarette and Tush shit him up one day and say he does only smoke zut like he father. From that time the fella only out to jumbie me and Tush. But things take a turn for the worse two weeks since me and Callender had a blowout and I cut he ass sound sound.

After that, I change my movements. I doing everything different for the last two weeks. I coming to school late and leaving early – lunch time, sixth period, third period. He couldn't chart me at all. If he want to ketch me it have to be in school, and he know he can't handle me in a handfight. So this kind of soft man thing to get me in trouble with the principal is he revenge? It make sense.

"Sir, whoever was in the room with Shelly Ann, wasn't me, sir." I know he ain't believe me, I not expecting him to believe me. But I know he ain't believe Shelly Ann neither because everybody in the school know that she does lie through she teeth. And too besides, even if me and she was in the room, she does take man for money. Pollard know that, everybody know that. So he have to decide if to believe Callender. Pollard smarter than that. He ain't going and punish nobody on Callender evidence, I sure about that.

Pollard ask Shelly Ann to excuse we and if you see she – she zesting up sheself, pushing out she chest and watching me hard like if cut-eye could do me something. To tell you the truth, I feeling sorry for she. I don't know what Tush and them fellas see in she. She is only sixteen but she does look like if she done live a lifetime already. Shelly Ann does boast and tell everybody how she does run things home, because since she was in Junior Sec she have boyfriend and now she mother can't tell she what to do. Tush went Junior Sec with she and he say that she get break out from real young. He tell me how she does charge fellas ten dollars at a time to arrange brush for them with a cousin she have who is twelve years old and in Standard Five.

Anyway, Shelly Ann leave and me and Pollard alone in the office.

"Look, Saleem…" he begin but I stop him.

"Not meaning to cut you, sir, but we wasting time here. I really ain't do nothing."

"I'm not suspending you. It's her word against yours. What I want you to do for me is keep a low profile for the next few days, please."

"That's it?"

"Yes, that's it. The talk on the compound is that you and Callender had some sort of altercation and he is looking to get back at you. So be on your guard."

When I reach out the office, Singh and De Freitas stand up, watching me and grinning. Singh elbow De Freitas and say loud enough for me to hear, "That is the kind of slackness you expect. Is only black people children you catching in them foolishness so." De Freitas still smiling with him, like he ain't realize he and all black getting shit up from Singh.

I brush past him and head down the corridor to find Tush and give him the score. In my mind I planning how the two of we have to deal with Callender. Tush is a man go hit Callender with level talk and Callender just can't take that and then he go look to fight; that is precisely where I go come in, because once he rush in on Tush, is a given I go have to swing for my partner. I done seeing in my head how Callender getting he next beat down when I realize them two security imps actually following me down the corridor and throwing talk for me. Singh singing the same tune as usual: nigger people this, nigger people that. De Freitas, like he ain't know better, only echoing Singh. Then Singh make a mistake and get personal. He start up on my mother. Saying how she have to be real worthless and how fruit don't fall far from tree, and that is how I come out worthless, too. One thing I don't walk away from is mother talk. Once you start up on my mother your cut ass book. I turn around and I watch Singh. I not like Tush, I ain't good at giving talk. The most I could do is cuss and is not cuss alone I want to cuss Singh. I want to cut him down, make him feel small. Make him know what it is to have people around watching you, while you wishing the ground could open up and take you. I want him to know how it does be when you feeling small. My mother worthless? My mother worthless? I watch the fucker hard and proper and decide before I dead I go do for the bitch.

So when I reach this morning, one time is look I looking for Tush to show him the gun and tell him my plan. But I can't find him. Nobody ain't see him in Block C. I went down in the Agri building and spot Marlon.

"Aye, boy, you see Tush."

"Last time I see him was by the science labs."

That ain't sound right, but I ain't have no reason to disbelieve so I make a tack back. No Tush. I went by the café and lime.

"Yeah, m'boy, I see Tush this morning. By the taxi stand. I ain't know if he come to school yet."

"Who's that? Tush? Yeah man, Tush come. I mean he reach." And a whole set of fellas start to laugh at that. Anything to do with sex, them find it funny.

"Where you see him?"

"Block C."

Then the fella stop taking me on because a girl that he like walk up.

It didn't make no sense to go Block C again, so I figure I go just wait for first period when we have Maths. Bell ring and I hear them fellas saying we have general assembly this morning. One time I decide I passing on that.

"Where we going?"

"Tech Voc Block, boy; it have plenty place to hide."

So about six of we head down there, passing behind Block E so the deans and them wouldn't see we. When we reach down, we settle on a concrete bench in the back of the building and put a fella name Taylor as lookout. One time a next fella name Jeremy start to roll a joint. Fellas start to grin. Even me, because was almost a whole day since the last time I roll one.

"Boy this is the real shit you know. I thief it from my brother. Grade A. I take a drag. One drag last night and ketch it. I ain't lying." He lick the paper, twist the ends and light up. The smell was sweet. He pass it and rock back. The fella he pass it to take a drag and start to cough.

"Boy, this thing real fucking strong." He take a next pull

and pass the joint. By the time all of we take two pull we was flying. Jeremy was right; it was Grade A for truth, it wasn't no press weed. Taylor get so high he stop looking out and start to make up stories about the last time he get high and the rest of them fellas join in. Everybody making up stories about all kind of madness. How they climb lamppost and tree and start to bark like dog and shit. All of them like they in a competition to see who does catch the worse head when they smoke.

Me, I just sit down mellow, feeling the weed pass through me, feeling light and easy, so light I forget about how heavy the gun is. My mind run on Tush. Tush should've been here. I like to get high round Tush; he does talk real shit. If he was here I woulda show him the gun and tell him what I planning to do and we woulda laugh like hell because he woulda see the humour in it. He woulda see how important it was to me. But while I sitting there flying, the shout went up.

"Deans! Fellas, Hillman and them coming."

Hillman is a dread Dean. He and the security and them is real partners and if the security and them like prison officers, Hillman is the governor. Give Hillman a chance and he tell you is he and not Pollard running the school. Men start to scatter. We went round the corner looking to hide. The best place for that is in the technical vocational rooms. All them classroom full of equipment for welding and plumbing and carpentry and thing. Jeremy and two fellas run into the joinery room. I head straight for the welding room because I know it have compressor to hide behind. I duck down and wait. I hearing Hillman and them coming; their footsteps stop and start, stop and start and I know is search they searching the rooms and them. I hear two fellas cry out and I know they get catch. I ain't worried.

Them fellas will take blows rather than sell out men because they know if they sell any of we out is real horrors. So I waiting, crouch up behind the compressor.

I hear them coming in and trying hard to breathe quiet and come back to earth because the weed still in my system. I hearing their foot coming closer and closer. They checking the welding booths. Anytime now they will reach the compressors. I crouch down more and then I hear a voice, De Freitas, say, "Look I seeing a school shirt across in the carpentry room. Let we check that out." I wait until they footsteps die down and I step out from behind the compressors grinning to myself because I real lucky. Same time I hear a noise and look to duck down again, but it wasn't a guard it was Jason Callender. He coming out from behind a compressor and Shelly Ann right with him. I pull myself square one time. Thing like coincidence I don't really believe in. Jason watching me aggressive but at the same time I know he know the guards and them still close by.

"This welding room smelling real stink, boy." I know is me Shelly Ann throwing that talk for, but I stay quiet.

"Somebody must be have their mother dirty hijab in they bag."

"Why you ain't hush yuh cunt." It slip out. I was thinking it but I didn't plan to say it. I know they was just trying to get me vex.

One time, because she man around, Shelly Ann try to rush me. But if the two of them feel I was going to let them beat me they lie. I have a gun and a knife. I breaks Shelly Ann cuff and let go a slap on she. Callender rush me and both of we fall down on the floor. I trying to get him off me and reach for the knife that strap around my leg, but Shelly Ann trying to get me in a headlock, so is both of them I contending with. In all this confusion chair and table falling over and banging up and next thing you know De Freitas and Singh on top the three of we and pulling we off each other. De Freitas holding me and Shelly Ann and Singh grappling with Callender. He break away from Singh and rush back at me and I reach for my knife one time. He jump back.

Singh bawl, "But ay ay! Look how them nigger quick to kill each other nah! Is girl the two of you fighting over? But Shelly Ann, you have real thing, girl!" Even I could see why Singh think is Shelly Ann have we fighting. De Freitas let go Shelly Ann and tighten he grip on me. Singh tell him, "Leave that one with me and take these two by the principal. Is straight suspension for them and I feel this one might get expel."

De Freitas shove me over to Singh and he grab the knife from my hand, spin me around so my back to him and he twist my arm behind my back. One time I feel the baton between my legs and tears start to full up my eye.

"All you niggers is real hell you know." He breath was hot, hot by my ears. "You smelling of weed, boy. So you smoking and you have weapon on you? Boy, today you out of school, boy. Is only all yuh niggers in this kind of slackness, yes." He carrying on with he nigger talk and squeezing my balls and I trying to get away. Because I know is a suspension I heading for and I know when Mammy hear this she go cry, because I is she last boy – the only one who look like he might finish school and I know once I get suspended she ain't sending me back. So I figure I go run, jump the fence and lie low for a few days and then come back in school. By that time them guards done forget about me.

But this Singh fella like he out for me, because he still have the baton between my legs and my hands behind my back and talking.

"We go have to call in police for this one, boy. Weapon involve. Possession with intent. It must be all you nigger children, eh? How much like you your mother make, eh? About six, seven? One after the other? Every year like a bitch in heat? All you have the same father? You even know who your father is?"

But he make a mistake. All the time he talking, he bending me forward and I reach down with my free hand and pull the gun. When I turn round on him I know I catch him because the nigger talk stop and he eye open big. He stretch out a hand and the talk change now because the power change. I in charge. Gun is a thing like that, it does change situations real easy. All of a sudden Singh ain't bad no more; I is the big sawatee and he blinking and looking stupid. He wondering what going on and I stand up quiet quiet, looking at him. Weighing my options, deciding what to do. How long to make him sweat before I make to dive off the compound. Because I know after this gun thing, I can't come back to school. The principal go be on my case and Singh go look to kill me. But I enjoying myself watching the coolie bitch sweat. Looking nervous, nervous and trying to talk me out of doing anything foolish.

"But ay ay," I tell him, "is only foolishness a stupid nigger like me capable of." I know he regretting all the nigger talk now.

But the gun fool me. I focus on it so much I lose track of everything. I didn't notice when Singh attitude start to change and he stop talking fast, fast, and the look in he eye went from frighten to mean. He start to look like the normal Singh again. Like he ain't fraid me or the gun. Something tell me look behind me and I realise De Freitas stand up there ready to swing a baton on my head and I duck and looking to run, but he grab me and I swing my hand and point the gun at him to frighten him and get the upper hand, because it ain't have no bullet in it. I can't afford one. De Freitas look to breaks and that is when I feel it, a sharp pain in my back!

A bullet not exactly like a knife eh, but it does cut still. Your flesh does have to move and make way for it and it have a kind of cold heat about it. It chilling you and burning you at the same time. My head hit the floor hard. My whole body. But things happening so fast and I feeling so hot and cold I not sure what going on. I touch my stomach, because that is where I feeling hot and cold the most. But is when I feel the stickiness it hit me. Where Tush, boy? I try to push myself up to see if I see Tush. I have to tell him something.

As I struggling to get up I see Singh watching me and I seeing something in he face because he watching me hard hard. He eyes digging me, but he ain't saying nothing. The words was right there in he eyes though. I coulda almost hear he voice saying, *Is I do this to you, nigger boy*.

REDEMPTION

New Testament Revival Tabernacle was only ten houses away from the Sunrise Palace Hotel and Bar. Redemption, the village in which these two places are situated, is really small. If you lived in Port of Spain you would say Redemption is pure bush, and the people there are country bookies who ain't exposed to much, and life have a sameness to it that could stifle you. So it's not surprising that the closeness of these two places is a constant source of talk. Even people who are just passing through talk about how these two places are positioned. The men talk about it and smile that kind of cunning smile they have when sex is the subject matter. The women talk about it, too, or complain rather, with shock in their voices, as if sex and God don't mix. But their real problem with these two buildings is that they know precisely who the patrons are.

You might also think it made sense for these establishments to be so close to each other because they had plenty in common. Both places were fully air-conditioned and serviced almost the same set of clients. The cars you saw parked at Sunrise on Friday and Saturday nights were the same ones parked at New Testament on a Sunday morning – their occupants now making a joyful noise unto the Lord. So it was nothing strange to hear cries like "Sweet Jesus!" or "Oh God!" in both buildings as folk raised their voices in a crescendo of praise to the gifts of life given by their Maker.

The owners of the cars paid their tithes at both places, religiously. It was either $40 an hour or one-tenth of their monthly earnings. Either way, they felt it was a small contribution to make for the joy that came into their lives. Neither place really discriminated against the customers of the other. The New Testament pastor, Winston Duncan, had learnt a long time ago the wisdom of judging not, lest he be judged, especially when his judgments started to affect the amount of money offered at collection. Those in the flock who were willing to throw a crisp hundred dollar bill in the collection plate at the end of the Sunday morning service expected and got the indulgence of a blind eye turned to at least one of their faults. Similarly, in his role as caretaker for his own particular flock of sinners, Mr Faustin, the owner of Sunrise, never turned anybody away unless all of the rooms were filled, and even then, once you were a regular customer, he would organize to clean up a back room quickly for you.

It's easy to understand why Sunrise was so popular. Redemption village is not a place with too much recreation. You could drink, play cricket or football, lime by the corner or run women. If you were able to do all three comfortably, then you became a hero in the village. It meant that as a man your business was in order and you had everything under control. You were a god among mortals.

Women, though, had rather less recreation allowed to them. There were the occasional church bazaars or harvests; sometimes the football or cricket club would host a family day; or there would be the informal gathering in someone's yard to exchange gossip. But mostly it was the routine of domestic chores that kept the women occupied.

Today though, the worlds at both ends of the street were coming together to celebrate the passing of one of their own. Stanton Crewley, one of the most respected men in Redemption village had died at Sunrise and now, three days later, was being buried at New Testament.

If there was a man in the village whom the younger men looked up to and tried to emulate it was Stanton. He was big and strapping and had a good job working as an installation technician for a telecommunications company. His wife, Sylvia, had been the catch of the day in her time. All the men had secretly or openly lusted after her, but Stanton had been the only one to stir real interest, the only young man to make it to her front porch and not only survive, but find favour with the village princess. As a boy he was the crowned prince. As a man he became the King. And now the monarch lay dead.

The way Stanton died gave the whole process of mourning a rare kind of excitement that lasted until the day he was buried. It was almost like a mini-series for Redemption. The incident was, of course, too trivial to require actual television cameras and reporters, but in its own way, Redemption afforded the key players in the tragedy their fifteen minutes of fame, though some were reluctant to accept it. From the morning he died to the day of the funeral, everybody had either a new piece of information to add to the story, or something to speculate about. Everybody waited patiently to see how things would play themselves out.

Mrs. Stanton, ever the lady, remained quiet and dignified throughout the affair. She knew that the mourners were there more to observe how she was dealing with the shame and strain than to offer any real condolences. Even the well-meaning ones, the ones she could usually rely on, were there carefully searching her face for the slightest flicker or change in expression to add to their stories. But Sylvia disappointed them. She served her Crix, coffee and sweetbread with the same expression she wore in New Testament on a Sunday: serene and poised. Eventually people got fed up of shoo shooing in the yard and went out into the road where they could voice their thoughts more openly and relish the gossip like a well-seasoned stew-chicken leg.

Down in Sunrise, the whole yard was lit up with flambeaux; even Room 12, where the ambulance had picked him up. Downstairs in the bar, men were ordering a Heart Attack, the new drink they had concocted since Stanton's passing. The village was like that; every occasion had to be marked with a name. If a flu virus had been going around at the time, they might have called it the "Stanton".

All five of the rumshops in Redemption were hot with talk about what lead up to his death.

"But boy, for a strapping fella like Stanton to get a heart attack, she had was to be real good!"

This was quickly followed by, "You ain't know if he heart was okay. Suppose he had a weak heart."

This was followed by a wave of sceptical laughter.

"Stanton weak?"

"You have to be joking! A big strapping man like Stanton? Who never feel sick a day in he life? Who had woman from since he old enough to make thing with them? All you have to be joking."

"Men like Stanton does live until they ninety. With children, grandchildren and great-grandchildren all over the damn place."

"Boy, men like Stanton does just get up good good one day and drop down dead just so."

For a moment there was silence. Men started to think about their health, their lives, the families they would be leaving behind. But as the next round of drinks arrived, the talk went back to Room 12 and the level of exertion that must have taken place for Stanton to die so scandalously.

In spite of all the talk, there was one name people hardly mentioned and when they did, they lowered their voices in an almost reverential way, the way a Catholic might make the sign of the cross when discussing something particularly sacred or evil. But this death, had turned Precious, who was already a legend in Redemption, into something almost mythical.

Precious's story had a kind of magic to it that thrilled the villagers. She'd arrived in Redemption at the age of fourteen, from Venezuela via Cedros. The owners at Sunrise had secured a forged birth certificate to say she was eighteen, in case the police ever made a raid on the premises and asked uncomfortable questions. The issue of her age caused heated arguments in the village. Sometimes even the midday television soap opera the women watched religiously was forgotten for a discussion about her age. Even Pastor Duncan raised it as a sermon in his pulpit. But when the Sunday after that saw a decline in the male attendance, Pastor called a halt to the fire and brimstone he was calling down on Sunrise and its owners. The women, though, still had plenty to say about Precious and her youth, because they knew their husbands had been with her.

It was difficult to say what Precious was. She looked Spanish, which was what everyone in Redemption assumed she was, but not quite Spanish. The men speculated that perhaps she had Amerindian blood. Whatever, it was the first time that anyone as exotic had been to Redemption.

"Snake oil waist" was what the men called her. Faustin organized things at the club with flair. He had seen how the clubs in the city did things and tried to copy them. Precious used to do a kind of pre-show whose purpose was to demonstrate not only that she was young, but also extremely flexible. Faustin would walk around while she was performing, asking the men if their wives could do any of the things Precious did. She would whip the men into a frenzy and would go to the highest bidder. Rumours flew about her insatiability.

Precious's stock was high. Men were lining up to conquer her or simply be able to say that they had possessed her. Stanton had not been one of them, though. His pleasure was the live show and once in a while, after a few drinks he might have fun with one of the girls. He never stayed overnight at the hotel. In his mind it was a big insult to his wife to be coming from another woman's bed in the early hours of the morning. Sylvia knew all of this. There was a quiet understanding between them. No public shame or embarrassment and all would be well. She understood her duty to him and he to her. Many times she would cross paths with one of the women from the hotel at the market and ignore her, back straight, nose held high. They borrowed her husband from time to time, but she was secure in her position as wife.

That was until the night Stanton decided that Precious was going to be his. His sudden passion for her caught him off guard. It was Faustin who explained it to the men.

"Boy, one night he bounce she up by the bar and buy she a drink and sit down in one long conversation, and then went upstairs with she. Then he was back the next night, then the next night, then the next night again. Like he had a fever and she was the bush tea."

At first, Mrs. Stanton gave no hint that she'd noticed a

change in his habits. She felt that, given time, things would settle and return to routine. Her mother had often told her, "Men does like to do their thing and have their own way. You just be patient. They does always come back. You is he married wife. He bound to come back."

The first time, on a Friday, when Stanton returned at daybreak instead of his customary midnight, she took note but remained quiet. He also managed to return just after midnight on Saturday, more than enough time to sleep and prepare for church the next day. By the following weekend, Stanton's behaviour was under scrutiny not just from his wife but the macos on the street.

Celestine John and Miss Agnes lived on either side of the Stantons. They had started their own surveillance, meeting at least twice in the day, just after *The Young and The Restless* and before *Santa Barbara*, to discuss the latest developments. They were waiting for Sylvia to open up and make some kind of a distress signal before they jumped in to console her. They didn't want to appear pushy and nosy. They noted that, on Sunday, Mrs. Stanton's amens in church did seem a little louder and to have more meaning than usual. But they were disappointed. Not once did Mrs Stanton ever discuss Precious with them, even when it was obvious that everybody else was talking about what was going on.

If ever a man was under a spell, it was Stanton. He went from spending all weekend to all week long at Sunrise. The more nights he spent there, the colder and tighter Mrs. Stanton got, but still not a word. She couldn't be faulted on her role as mother and wife. The children and the house were in immaculate order, and she only stopped being a *complete* wife to Stanton from the moment he went to Sunrise one Friday night and only came home midday the following Saturday. Stanton made no comment, but his hours and behaviour became even more erratic. All he could be relied on to do was to take the family to church on Sunday.

While his status as husband was in peril, his position as village hero remained intact. The men were only too anxious to have him around, hungry to understand his madness even though they never spoke directly to him about Precious. That was not how it was done. Stanton was, after all, married. His wife was to be respected. But when he had finished his last drink with them, or got up to leave at the end of a card game, they didn't press him to stay; they understand that he had an agenda and needed to attend to it.

He never used the word love in the presence of his closest friends, but it was there all over his face on the few occasions he mentioned her name. At first it was only the sex he talked about. Her softness and flexibility and eagerness to please him. Never any headaches or tiredness. But after a while his obsession became plain. The way he talked, it was as if he was the only man she had been with, ever. The men were shocked.

"The man mashing up he good good living for a piece of skin!" was Boboy's comment. "I never know Stanton to be getting on tootoolbay so! The man does usually have heself in order."

The others in the bar silently agreed, happy that though they had tasted of Precious, they weren't infected with the same madness.

And while Stanton was hot and sweaty with Precious, some of the more enterprising men had begun to pursue Mrs. Stanton. They were ignored. She treated them to a cold, unseeing stare when they approached her at the market or the shop or even on the side of the road, pretending to want to help her and then propositioning her in their sly way. They took their rebuffs quietly. To protest would draw attention to themselves, especially from Stanton. As occupied as he was with Precious, Sylvia was still his property.

For a time, it appeared as if Stanton had recovered control of himself. One of his sons fell ill. Stanton was back at the house, no longer frequenting Sunrise as he made regular trips to the hospital in the city to visit his son. Weeks passed in this way until one night a drunken rumshop customer hailed him out saying, "Boy, I woulda say Precious mighta dry up and dead after you stop coming round Sunrise, but the girl bloomin man. Business swinging!"

If Stanton's skin had been lighter, he might have paled. That night he and Precious fought in public like a regular married couple. Faustin had to put him out and Stanton became the first customer to be refused access to Sunrise. The story went that he had rushed into the place and gone straight up to Room 12, interrupting Precious and a client. He had dragged Precious out, with only a sheet protecting her, even roughed her up a bit, all the while shouting, "You promise me! You promise me!"

The news spread like bush fire that night. By the time neighbours started sweeping their yards next morning, everyone on Stanton's street had the score. Mrs. Stanton pretended she didn't notice how people were watching and whispering as she sent her other son off to school and prepared to go to the hospital.

Stanton began to lose his position in Redemption. At work he became the butt of malicious jokes and endless picong. Men would randomly begin conversations about fighting in public or how stupid some men behaved over women. To Stanton's credit he took the talk, but even he realized that he had fallen from grace. The men around him had found their hero was weak: a woman had conquered him.

"Poom poom rule, boy!" men called in the rumshops. They didn't bother to lower their voices if Stanton was around. In fact, if anything, they talked louder, relishing the effects of their comments. Things got so bad that one evening Stanton threw a cuff behind Boboy; they scuffled in the rumshop and had to be parted. But Stanton had fought only to save face. Now when he entered any of the rumshops he would walk straight to a corner table and sit only with his closest friends. The days of him walking into a bar to loud greetings and calling for a round of drinks were over.

About two weeks after the fight at Sunrise, Stanton moved Precious into an apartment. That raised so much talk, even the Pastor preached on it. Stanton wasn't present for that sermon. Still Mrs. Stanton said and did nothing. Her quietness became quite alarming. People started speculating that the pressure of staying quiet over something so shameful must be sending her mad.

Stanton barely went home anymore. He visited on weekends, cleaned the yard and spent awkward time with his children. The boys either ignored him or sat down and watched him with sour faces because their mother told them they had to spend time with him.

The women were waiting in their own agony for a showdown between Mrs. Stanton and Precious. Miss Agnes got so impatient she asked Mrs. Stanton point blank what she was going to do. The women in Redemption began to feel let down. Not only had she lost her man – which could happen to any of them – she had lain down and taken it – no fight, no struggle.

One Saturday their paths finally crossed at the market;

Mrs. Stanton moved quietly towards a heap of cucumbers while Precious continued to haggle over the price of yams. The whole market waited on tenterhooks wondering what would happen next. When they realized that nothing would happen, that in fact, Mrs. Stanton was quietly skittering away while Precious held her ground, a dam burst.

"But she is a blasted fool. Any woman could just take my man and get away so?"

"Me is one woulda mash up their apartment long time and buss up she ass!"

"Imagine, a good-looking woman like Sylvia eh, is not to say she is any old fowl, a nice red woman like Sylvia have this mix-up Spanish bitch mashing up she living so!"

"Me, I woulda done dead from shame. But look how Sylvia just taking this cool. Like she ain't even noticing what going on. If she ain't mad I ain't know what wrong."

"Poor thing, though. To have to deal with all this in such a short space of time. In less than a year she gone from queen of the village to a damned fool. Everybody laughing at she behind she back, some even laughing in she face and still not a peep from she. She don't even try to defend she reputation. Playing Miss High and Mighty. She feel she too good to touch all this nastiness, when the nastiness coming from she own house. She have to deal with this whether she want to or not. The time will come when she ain't have no choice but to face it."

"Sylvia ain't moving like a woman there at all, she moving like a damned cunumunu, bébé bébé like she is a damned child. She allowing the two of them to set she pace. She moving scared, scared."

"And you believe she still referring to the man as husband? I hear that when Sunday come she does still set the table with a place for him! She saying she doing it for the children. Children! Children, my ass! Them children ain't have time for he, they ain't want to see their father, 'cause he hurt them. Sylvia know in she heart of hearts she still want him. She still waiting for him to give up the woman and come back. I does feel sorry for woman who grow up like Sylvia, because she have a mother who tell she it okay to take all this shit from a man and stay quiet."

"You give she wrong, Celestine. Stanton is she man. Look how much years she give him before this woman come in the picture? Eh? You think is just so you does give up a husband? And say what you want, he still minding she and the children. Bill still paying and food still reaching on the table. In he own way he still loyal to the family."

"But just so, the man practically shack up with this next woman. You woulda take that quiet so in your young days, Miss Agnes? Mr Bertille coulda ever come back home after he do you something like that?"

Then just as quickly as the affair started, it ended. It didn't make any sense. People were confused. One Monday evening, after work, Stanton turned up at his house instead of going to the apartment that he and Precious shared, parked his pick-up in its usual position under the mango tree and went into his house. Precious returned to Sunrise. The news ran as fast as it could up and down the street. By the following Sunday morning, New Testament Tabernacle could barely contain itself with all the talk.

There was a noticeable shifting and nudging in the pews when the family arrived, Stanton in front, head high, leading his pride down the aisle towards the Lord. Pastor had a hard time getting the murmuring down as he started the service. The first song he chose was clearly a test for Stanton: "Yield Not to Temptation". The congregation tittered through the organ's opening bars, waiting for the verse to start. All eyes were on Stanton and he didn't disappoint. With his eyes looking at the rafters, he belted out the chorus: "Yield not to temptation, for yielding is sin... Look ever to Jesus, He will carry you through." His voice led the congregation for the entire song. With the closing bars he looked around, challenging the congregation to mock him or continue to titter. The king had returned.

The men were the first to seal the unspoken truce, seeking him out in the courtyard to shake his hand and say a respectful hello to Mrs. Stanton, who stood quietly next to Stanton with her children. The women, less ready to forgive but having no choice, followed suit, though from the looks they exchanged and the couyou mouths they were making, you knew they would meet later to chew over the story.

Life went back to normal. Stanton was at home with his wife and children and Precious was making money for Faustin. The men who visited her were careful not to mention her name in front of Stanton. Once or twice they slipped and his face would go still. There would be a rush of conversation to cover the awkwardness. The only change was that Stanton never returned to Sunrise. Not even for a round of drinks with the boys. Until the night he died.

Nobody saw it coming. The men had settled at Sugar's Rumshop after an impromptu cricket game. The match fell apart after Boboy got run-out and refused to accept it. Stanton had made a violent pelt towards the stumps and long after the match had ended was complaining about cramps running up and down his left arm.

A noisy group made their way off the field, by turns complimenting and criticizing each other's performance. Eventually the conversation turned to more philosophical talk about life and family. Boboy started it after a deep pull on a bottle of beer.

"Boy, you think after marriage and children you go feel settled, eh? I married bout fifteen years now, have two children and it does still feel like it supposed to have something else. Something more."

"I know what you mean," chimed in Clement. "When I was in school I used to think that to be a policeman had to be the best thing in the world. It couldn't have nothing better than that. To walk down the street in your uniform, swinging your baton, gun hook in your side, people watching you with respect. I have all of that and it come like nothing. Then I say to myself, 'Clement boy, you need to get a wife, settle down, make some children. I do all of that and still… still I don't feel…" he paused as if searching for his thoughts, "I don't feel like my life full up. I don't feel full up. Sometimes I does think maybe is a promotion I need. A change of pace. But after that, then what?"

"Boy, sometimes I think it ain't have a thing like satisfied and happy. I think we could only *make do* with what we have, and once in a while, when we having a good lime, or we and we woman enjoying weself and things good and the talk nice, maybe then we could think we happy. But I don't think it possible to really be satisfied one hundred percent and be happy all the time. If I happy, really happy, three, four times in a year I glad for that. What you say there, Stanton?"

Stanton sat quietly, almost as if unaware a question had been asked, his right arm still massaging his left shoulder while he stared at the drink in front him. His face looked funny, a cross between sadness and pain. Clement tried to prompt him again, but Stanton got up and left, mumbling an excuse. There was a awkward silence until the conversation resumed, but this time the men talked of minor things, conscious that somehow they had rubbed Stanton the wrong way.

The wail of an ambulance siren in the wee hours of the morning warned people that somewhere in Redemption things were bad for somebody. Some turned long enough in their beds to wonder who in the village was sick enough to need an ambulance at this hour of the morning, then fell back to sleep, confident that the news would get to them later in the morning.

The following night the men heard the details from Faustin.

"The man come in here drunk and kind of desperate looking, calling for Precious. I did always feel he woulda come back for she, you know. I had to beg him to quiet down, because she was with a customer. I call she, without telling she who it is asking for she. When she reach downstairs and see him, the two of them just watching each other quiet. He open he mouth like he was going to start to say something and quiet quiet she tell him, 'Hush, we could talk upstairs.' They went upstairs – mind you he ain't pay down nothing eh – and the next time I hear bout him is when she tell me we need an ambulance."

"He look sick at all?"

"No, he look normal. Just a little drunk and sad. But he didn't look sick. Precious say he was complaining about he shoulder cramping, but that was about it."

Stanton's funeral was a holiday for Redemption. Hardly anybody went to work because it was scheduled for 11 am, and those who went to work signed their time sheets and left early. From Mrs. Stanton's living room to under the trees in her yard was packed with people who had come to get a glimpse of the body and see if he looked any different. Some came away from staring at him in his powder-blue suit, swearing he had a smile on his face. Outside in the yard, far away from the women, the young men joked that he probably still had an erection and that was probably why only half the casket was open.

The crowd walked along with the hearse the two streets from Stanton's house to New Testament. Some of them were hoping the car would have passed in front of Sunrise. Rumour had it that Precious was planning to attend, but the driver, sensitive to the scandal, had taken a different route.

In the church, everybody was united in their grief, singing, swaying and praying for Stanton's spirit to reach heaven safely. Mrs. Stanton leaned on her sons, singing and dabbing her eyes. That was when Precious and a few others from Sunrise came in at the back of the church. Their outfits alone told you they were not accustomed to grieving. People tangled their heads to see, some staring openly as the news made its way to the front of the church that Precious was present.

Pastor Duncan was inviting people to come up and say a word or two of remembrance for Stanton, or even to sing a song. Stanton's last remaining aunt, Miss Evey, came and talked about his childhood. How he had really loved cricket, breadfruit oil-down and life, and how saddened she was to see him cut down in his prime. Clement, who nominated himself as best friend that day, talked about their schooldays, their weddings, their lives as grown men. Stanton's boss came and acknowledged him as a real leader among the men. The eldest son maintained that in spite of everything, Daddy had taken good care of them and their mother loved him and missed him. It was as he spoke about his mother's enduring love for his father that Mrs. Stanton let loose a long, hoarse wail. It was what the women had been waiting for. At last they could do what they had wanted to do for so long – give Sylvia comfort and collectively absorb her misery. They knew that it was not grief at Stanton's passing that caused the tears; if anything it was relief from the burden of his horning ways. Their hands reached forward, handkerchiefs and bottles of Limacol and smelling salts at the ready.

In all the commotion, no one noticed when Precious left her seat and took the microphone away from Miss Evey who was leading the choir in a rendition of "Are You Washed in the Blood of the Lamb".

Her voice was tentative at first.

"I want to say something about Stanton." Then she stopped as if she wasn't sure if she should continue or even be there. The congregation watched in a menacing way, as if they wanted to beat her. Some mothers covered their children's faces, as if watching Precious was a sin in itself.

"I hear all of you talk bout Stanton. About how you know him, and love him and really miss him." She paused again looking at the casket in front of her. "I know what all of you here think of me. But in spite of all of that, I want to stand here and say that I miss and I love Stanton, too."

A chorus of steups followed the statement and a murmur started up.

"Who the hell she think she is? Love! Love! She live with the man for a few months and she could talk about love. Try living with him for twenty years, making he children, living with him everyday, taking the pressure and taking horn whenever he feel like it."

But Precious remained strong.

"I not here for your approval. I just want to say that in

spite of everything Stanton was a good man. The best man I know. He was the only man who ever, in all the time I living here in Redemption, see me as a person. All you see me only as a whore. Something to use or to hate from a distance.

The congregation nearly collapsed at her boldness. The murmuring got louder. The women were angry that what was supposed to be Mrs. Stanton's moment was being upstaged. Here was Precious getting on more like the grieving widow than the widow herself.

"But with Stanton I wasn't just a whore. He see… saw me as a person. He know I had hopes and dreams. I know he had hopes and dreams too. I know all the things he wanted to do with his life. He helped me to realise I could have goals too."

Sensing just how vexed people were getting she sped up.

"I just wanted all of you, well really Stanton, to know, that I love him and I really appreciate all he was to me."

She walked down the aisle to the casket and kissed Stanton's cheek.

There was a low groan, followed by a slight scuffle, as Precious stood bent over Stanton. Mrs Stanton broke loose from the cocoon of women and headed straight for her, arms arcing wide. As Precious raised up, she let loose a slap on her. Women screamed and the prostitutes at the back stepped out of their pew ready to defend their own. But Precious motioned them back.

Mrs Stanton was heaving from the effort of the slap and watching Precious like she wasn't sure what to do next.

"I know you hate me and I understand why. But I want you to ask yourself something? In all the time you was married to Stanton, you was ever happy to see him? So happy that as soon as you hear his voice you feel you could burst? If he wasn't the king of this village, if he wasn't the man that every other woman wanted, if he wasn't a good provider, if he was just some poor ketch-ass man with the same hopes and dreams, would you been happy to see him when he came home? You woulda love him at all? Because Stanton tell me that you never love him. He tell me he never feel like it was love. He tell me you love what he represent to you, but you don't love him. He wasn't happy with you. He was never happy with you. He say so. But he tried to make it with you. All he wanted you to do was to cherish him a little. Instead you treat him like he was some kind of plaque to put on display. He leave because he was fed up being a plaque on the wall of the house. It ever occur to you that it take more than a wedding ceremony and having children to make him happy? It ever occur to you that when he come home from work on evenings he wanted more than some food? That sometimes he wanted to talk about he and you, and not just the house and the children? You feel beating me in public will make you look like a good wife? Try it! But as much as I is a whore, I was more Stanton's woman than you ever could be!"

And that was the hardest slap right there. That lash was the one that Revival heard the loudest. Even after Precious and the rest of the prostitutes walked out the door, it left a ringing sound in people's ears. The women tried to comfort Mrs. Stanton but it was half hearted. She was a weakened woman. All of her practised poise and self-possession was gone. At the graveside behind New Testament, Stanton's sons threw in the first handfuls of dirt on his casket while his wife leaned up, crying on Celestine.

At the other end of the street, in Room 12, the candle that had remained lit for three days was blown out and a picture taken down from the dressing table. Life had to go on.

THE FAIREST OF THEM ALL

Ma vex with Rajin. He teacher send for she to come in school. She send the message with me today. She tell me to ask Ma come because Rajin using bad language.

Rajin beg me not to tell Ma. But I tell him I have to because if I don't, and the teacher tell Ma what she ask me to do, then both of we go get licks. Rajin real cry, but I still tell Ma.

Ma get vex one time when she hear. She start to cuss up Rajin.

"You just like your wutliss good-for-nothing father! All he ever do is drink rum and cuss, and now I have to go in school for you because you cussing. I only waiting to hear you start drinking rum and then I taking you out of school and you and your good-for-nothing father could saddle horse together."

Rajin get real upset too and after he change he clothes he leave the yard and go look for Ramesh and Kendall and the other boys he does play with. Them like some real musketeers. The three of them always together. Even in school. Is like they don't get to spend enough time with each other.

I tell Ma she shouldn' quarrel with Rajin so.

"Aye, Aye! So you telling me how to discipline my own child now? Eh?"

"No, Ma. But you boof him for cussing and then you cuss him. That ain't make sense."

Ma was in a real bad mood and when I tell she that, she ring my lip for rudeness.

Same time she do that, Silla walk in the house from school. Silla in evening shift in the Junior Sec where they does finish by half-past five, but everyday she coming home later and later. She walk straight to the bedroom. Ma get even more vex.

"But aye aye! Is only big man and woman I have in this house. Rajin cussing, you telling me how to raise my children and now Sushilla walk in here like she own the place. Not even a 'Good evening, Ma, how you do?' Look, Sushilla, pelt your little tail outside here!"

Silla come outside and she mouth swell up, swell up. These days Silla always vex. Ma say since she start Junior Sec she getting force-ripe. Once or twice she try to beat she, but Pa say leave she alone. Silla is Pa favourite. She could get away with murder with Pa. You would think the way how Pa like Silla, Silla would like him back, but she does get on like she don't care, don't care. When she in a good mood she talk to him. When she in a bad mood – leave she alone.

So Ma take a turn in Silla skin and Silla only stand up with she hand on she waist, shaking she hip. Ma real hate that. She start to advance on Silla like she want to slap she. Silla hit she one look and say, "Quarrel all you want, but don't slap me, because I will tell Pa."

"You will tell Pa! You will tell Pa! You see your Pa here? Eh?"

"He up the road by the shop. He go be here just now. Just wait."

And Silla flounce out the kitchen. That was Silla for you. Not even fourteen and she getting on like she, and not Ma, is the woman of the house.

When we was young Pa used to play a game with we. He

used to tell we fairy stories. Sometimes he make up things and put them in the story. When he tell us *Snow White* he used to make Silla Snow White and she get to say the 'mirror mirror on the wall' part in the story.

When we was growing up and Silla get vex, Pa used to tease she and ask, "Who is the fairest of them all, eh Silla, who is the fairest?" Silla would fight to keep she face serious, but then eventually she would smile. But not now though. Silla get real grown up since she hit Junior Sec. So I know when he reach home this evening and Ma finish giving him the story, he go have to find a next way to make Silla smile because he can't take it when Silla vex. When he going by the shop for he cigarette after dinner and he ask she to come and she say no, he face does fall and then he does beg she and promise to buy snack and thing for she. But if me and Rajin get vex it don't bother him so much.

Same time I going outside to wet the plants for Ma, I see Rajin coming back in the house. He face well set up and he fly in the room. I turn to tell him Silla there and he can't use the room. But he only steups at me. Everybody vex and taking it out on me.

I like wetting plants. The water does make all kind of patterns on the leaves and sometimes when I stare at the patterns for real long, my mind does go all over the place and think up all kinds of things. Sometimes I does think about all them fairy tales Pa used tell we and the ones we used to read in school. My favourite was *Puss in Boots*. If I could be in a fairy tale I would be Puss from *Puss in Boots*. He get to go all over the place.

I hear Pa whistling as he reach home. From the kitchen I hear Ma start to slam pot so I know they going to quarrel. I stay outside with the plants. It safer. Instead of going inside, though, Pa come around by the garden. I feel he was going by the shed to smoke. I afraid to go by that shed. Sometimes in the night I does hear noise from the shed like if spirit walking by it or shaking it. I don't know how Pa so brave to go and smoke by that shed all the time. Ma don't like it when he smoke inside. She say he just like them chimney in the factory he working in, and how he getting black just like them too.

"Evening, Pa."

"Evening, evening. You good, girl?"

"Yes, Pa."

"How school?"

"School good, Pa."

"You behaving yourself? Making your Pa proud?"

"Yes, Pa."

"You wetting them plants or playing in water?" He pull my ponytail with one hand and wring the tail of the shirt I was wearing so tight it squeeze my chest and all my navel was printing out. The shirt was soaked all the way through so water drip through his hands.

"I wetting the plants, Pa."

"Well, come inside fast before you catch a cold, eh." He was still holding my ponytail and playing with it.

"You getting a big girl now, Chandra, so you can't stay outside late. Your Pa have to watch out for you. It have people might take advantage of little girls outside they parents' house late."

There was a noise by the kitchen window. Silla was standing up watching us. Pa dropped my ponytail and turned to go inside.

"Ma say to tell you come." Silla was still sounding vex.

"She vex, nah?" Pa grumbled. "That woman always quarrelling. No peace for a man."

The quarrel real heat up in the kitchen. Ma start up on

Pa case one time, telling him how he useless and ain't helping she around the house, and how all he children following in he footstep because me and Silla rude and Rajin cussing in school. Silla and Rajin jump in to defend theirself one time.

"Pa, I say good evening and she didn't hear. She was boofing Chandra, so how she could hear?"

"I didn't cuss no bad word, Pa. You could come in school for yourself and ask Miss. I didn't cuss no bad word."

Pa get vex with all the noise and he start to cuss everybody. I turn off the hose and sit down outside. Then Pa say he going for cigarettes and he tell Silla to come with him. Silla look like she was going say no, but then Pa say he go buy she a soft drink.

Ma start to cry and bawl out behind him. "Watch you, you ass. Thing get hot and you run. You have your son and daughter getting on like man and woman in this house and when I tell you about it, all you could do is run to the shop and smoke."

I wait until the house get quiet before I go inside. Ma was sitting by the table cleaning bodi to cook in the morning. She was staring at the bodi but I could tell she wasn't really watching it. She face had a faraway expression. She look like how I feel when I thinking about travelling to see places, but sadder. I does feel sorry for Ma sometimes. She does look so tired and fed up. Then she look up at me.

"Child, look how you soak down! All your skin showing through your shirt. Like you want to catch a cold and give me more headache?"

"I going and change now, Ma."

She continued to stare at me. "You like your ma, eh, Chandra girl?"

"Yes, Ma."

"You saying that because you fraid I hit you?"

"No, Ma. I like you, Ma." She was looking sad.

"Sometimes I does feel none of you like me. Rajin playing man. Silla come big woman now. Pa don't help me. You and all getting big and rude."

"Ma, I not rude."

"Sometimes I does feel like I could leave. Go somewhere far. Forget all of this"

I walk off quiet quiet to the room. I didn't bother to turn on the lights but started to peel off my wet clothes, thinking about how Ma want to be like Puss in Boots and run off to a far place. I get so lost thinking I almost didn't hear Rajin.

"Get out boy, I changing."

"I can't see nothing, Chandra."

I hustled into my clothes. He was lying down on the bed with his back to me and he voice sound like if he was crying. I is eleven and Rajin nine. Ma used to bathe us and change us together when we was younger, but now that I and Silla is big girls and seeing we monthlies, she say he can't be in the same room when we changing.

"Ma go buss your tail when she hear you was in the room while I dressing."

"I don't care." He turned over to face me and continued to sniffle.

"But you fraid you get your tail cut tomorrow when Ma find out the bad word you use." He stay silent but continue to sniffle a little harder.

"What bad word you use?"

He had turned his back again and was almost talking into the pillow. "I didn't use no bad word. Miss lying on me."

"What stupidness you talking, Rajin? How Miss go lie on you? So when Ma turn up there tomorrow, your teacher going make up a story about how you cuss? Is not in front the class you cuss?"

"I didn't cuss."

"So, if you didn't cuss, what you say?"

"I say bull."

"What?" I could barely hear what he was saying. He move his head a little so the pillow wasn't in his face

"Bull."

"Like cow and bull?" He shift his head again and say something under his breath.

"What you say, boy? I ain't hear you."

Rajin take a breath and then he turn to me. "You know the man across the road from the school have a set of goat, right?" I nodded. "Well Suresh ask Miss where all them goats come from and I raise my hand and tell him when two goats bull they does make children, and that is where they come from."

"Where you learn that word?" I was in shock. When Ma reach in school and hear this, Rajin go be in real trouble.

"From Ramesh and Kendall."

"How come all you was talking about that?"

Rajin drop he head again.

"We was playing in morning recess and they tell me how last week they see two people bulling in the field behind the shop. I ask them what that mean and them real laugh at me and then they explain is big people does do it and that is how everything does make young one. They tell me we could go by the field later and check and see if we see the people and them there. Then I will know what bull is."

He was crying fully now, tears streaming down his face.

"Well you better save some of that cry for tomorrow. Ma go blaze your tail for using that dirty language."

He start to cry even harder. I feel sorry for him.

"Boy, shut up. If Ma hear you, she will feel I beating you."

He was quiet for a while, then he say, "It have more, Chandra."

The way he say it make me feel a little strange. Like if something real bad was going to happen.

"Chandra, you have to promise not to say nothing."

The bad feeling get even stronger.

"Boy, stop crying and talk fast."

"Chandra... you can't tell Ma."

"Can't tell Ma what? Talk fast Rajin." He was getting me real vex and the sick feeling was getting worse.

"Kendall and Ramesh carry me behind the shop. And I see a man..."

The idiot boy stop talkin'. My heart beating fast and my mouth dry and he just stop.

"Who is the man, Rajin?" I was almost shouting at him. At the same moment I hear Pa's voice in the kitchen. In the dim light of the bedroom I could see Rajin's eyes widen in fear and something else. Then it hit me.

"You see Pa?"

He nodded quickly and mouthed something.

"What?"

He mouthed it again. In the darkness I could barely make it out.

"Boy, talk fast."

"And..."

The door cracked open and Silla stepped in.

"What the two of you stand up in the dark here doing? Ma... Chandra and Rajin in the room by theirself in the dark and she changing she clothes!"

★

You shoulda see how guilty the two of them look stand up in the bedroom in the dark. Rajin telling Chandra something that he ain't want me to know about because as soon as I was in the room he shut up and they step apart from each other, start to find other things to do and put on the light. It look like Chandra was changing she clothes and the two of them know that he not supposed to be in the bedroom if one of we changing we clothes. Chandra encouraging slackness. Ma should buss up she tail. But Ma ain't go do that. Chandra is she eyeball. She always telling me how I force-ripe and how Chandra is the only one does listen to she, and how Chandra bright and doing well in school and bound to pass for Convent. The way Ma does carry on is like Convent is the be all and end all of everything. When I was doing exam to get into secondary school all she singing in my head was "Convent, Convent, Convent." If we passing anywhere near to a cloth store she checking to see if they selling uniform material for Convent. And when she talking to the neighbours and them, all you hearing is, "When Silla pass for the Convent, I go be so happy. Is plenty book she go have to carry to school. I hope she father bracing heself for the expense."

And when you see I ain't pass for this Convent is like I do Ma something. When I come home from school and tell she my results she real bawl.

"Junior Sec! Junior Sec, Silla! After all the study and sacrifice, Junior Sec!"

She was real vex and real sad. She couldn't bring sheself to tell the neighbours. But you know how neighbours is; they find out anyway. And I could tell from their face –

when they pretending they ain't know where I pass for – that they was happy that I pass for the Junior Sec. Some of their children self pass through the Junior Sec already. If I did pass for Convent, I would have been the first girl from we village to go there. It have a boy who pass for the boy college already. Everybody was real proud. If you see he parents and them now, like they can't mash ants. Everything is "Ravi say this" and "Ravi say that". Like since he start college he become a lord. And is like the teachers them in the college and the convent come like God self for Ma and the neighbours.

"Them nuns and priests don't make joke, you know."

"Is true. You have to beat books once you in them schools."

"They don't make joke when it come to discipline, you know. You see how them Junior Sec children does be lahay, lahay all over the place. You ain't getting that with them seven-years school. Them girls who going Convent ain't have time to study boys. And them boys have too much book to learn to take on girls."

You swear Ma and the neighbours went to Convent theyself. But Pa wasn't vex with me. He was the only person in the house who tell me congratulations and tell me he proud of me. He tell me he never get the chance to go secondary school.

"I drop out of primary school to learn mechanic. And since then that is all I doing. I lucky the factory did take me on to fix machine in their workshop. Don't study your Ma. She want good things for you, but she have a way where she figure she better than people, and she figure she children is the same way. Nothing wrong with the Junior Sec. Is the same schooling you go get there. Is the same Maths and English all the schools teaching."

Ma start to focus on Chandra more from then. Because the teacher tell she Chandra bright and Chandra have potential. Well, she could keep she Chandra, I have Pa. Pa love me more than he love all of them. He self tell me that.

After results did come out, all the children from my class spend a term in Standard Six. The teacher tell we is time to relax. She say after that term and the long holidays when school start back is real work in secondary school. So that term we get to learn to swim and play plenty games. I start my monthlies that same term. One day we playing catch in school and I fall down and my uniform raise up and the boys start to laugh and call me "Dirty panty". I real cry and when I went by Miss she ask me if I don't know about period. She give me a pad and tell me a little about it. Everything she say sound strange. I going and bleed for a few days every month? Why? To make children?

When I reach home that evening I tell Ma and the first thing she say is, "Already! Well, Lord, look how my troubles now start!"

I feel like I did do something wrong. Chandra ask me what was wrong and I couldn't explain it to she. She and all went and ask Ma what is a period, and Ma tell she she too force-ripe.

That same evening, after Pa reach home and he walking to go by the shop, Ma stop him from carrying me. You see how she spiteful? She know whenever Pa going to the shop he does carry me for the walk and buy snacks for me. All she tell him is, "She can't go, she sick."

Then Pa say, "Sick with what? She looking normal to me."

Ma steups and start to carry on about how if she say I sick, then I sick. So Pa went without me even though I stand up there and cry so that he wouldn't leave me.

After she cook that evening she tell me about the thing. But she sound so vex when she telling me. Like if I do something wrong. Like is my fault I bleeding.

"What you getting is a period. Every month it go come. It does come so when you is a big woman you could make a child. Don't let none of them little boys come around you. Because you will make a baby if that happen. Make sure and keep yourself clean. And if you getting pain let me know, okay. You will start to get breast too and hair under your arm and between you leg."

That was it. Some of the things she talk about, like the hair and breast I did know about. Is in school when I talking to the other girls that I find out more thing. Like the boy have to do more than be next to you. He have to touch you. But we didn't know how. One girl, Savitri, say that if they did touch we panties we would get pregnant. We was real stupid then.

A few days later I get to go in the shop with Pa. He ask me how I feeling. I tell him I good.

"Nothing wasn't wrong with me, Pa. I don't know why Ma tell you I sick."

"What you mean nothing wasn't wrong? Your Ma not mad."

"Pa, I wasn't sick, Pa." Then I tell him about the period. He look a little shock.

"You coming a big woman now, Silla. You have to be careful around the boys."

"That is the same thing Ma say."

"Well listen to your Ma and behave yourself. When we reach by the shop stick close to me, eh."

That period thing didn't come back the next month like Ma promise, or even the month after that. Eventually it start to come regular. Pa used to watch me. If I get the slightest belly pain he quick to ask me if I alright. Some-times Ma used to get vex. "Oh God, how you muching she up so? The slightest thing – 'Silla, you alright? Silla, you ok?' You have two other children you know!"

That is how Ma is. Any little attention you getting from Pa she vex. And is so the two of them always quarrelling. When she feel she ain't winning the argument she does start to cry for sympathy. And she always quick to tell Pa that he good-for-nothing and that she ain't bound to stay with him, she could always pack up and go back by she family and live peaceful there.

When she tell Pa them kind of thing so, he does go and sit down outside in the back by the shed and smoke cigarette. Sometimes he does go by the shop and smoke and drink with the men there. Then when he come back home drunk they does cuss and quarrel with each other even more until they go and sleep. Sometimes Pa does stay up long, long, long before he go and sleep. Is a night like that when he tell me how much he love me.

Sometime things does happen so fast, eh. You know in the five months between exam results and starting Junior Sec I get breasts. Enough for people to notice. So when we went to shop for uniform, Ma had was to buy bra for me too. You shoulda see Chandra face. She get so jealous when she see me putting it on when I was trying on my new uniform. Like Pa did know too. On my first day for school he give me a hug and tell me, "You is a big woman now, girl. Big school and thing. Do your best and watch out for the boys, eh."

That evening and every evening after that, Pa would wait out by the shop for me, where the taxi does drop you off, and he would walk me home, telling he friends this is he big daughter and, yes, I start big school.

All Ma say when she was leaving me by the school on the first day was, "Behave yourself and come straight home."

It had an evening when I reach the shop and Pa wasn't there. When I walk home I hear he and Ma quarrelling.

"You always by the shop and she always by the shop. If I didn't know better I would of say something going on. What going on?"

"Seema, how much time I go tell you. Nothing."

I know who they was quarrelling about. Like every month Ma does catch a vaps and take a turn in Pa tail about this woman who living close to we. She name Sushilla just like me and Ma feel the two of them have a thing going. Plenty time she tell him she know he horning her with the woman. Every time Pa does tell she no, but Ma does quarrel until she start to cry and Pa does have to much she up.

But Ma was in a real mood that evening. She pelt pot and thing and when Pa try to calm she down she tell him, "Take your half-dead self and go by your woman. Don't touch me." Pa look like he wanted to slap Ma. He leave the house and Ma went in she room and cry until she get quiet.

I went and look for Pa. He was smoking behind the shed. I sit down next to him.

After a while he say, "You see how husband and wife does fight like cat and dog? Don't get quarrelsome like your mother when you grow up, eh, Silla."

"No, Pa. I wouldn't get quarrelsome." Ma was too ignorant. Pa say so often. I wasn't going to get that way and be vex all the time.

"The way your mother does get on I does wonder why she married me. We wasn't no arrange marriage. We did married for love. But now I does wonder."

I feel real sorry for Pa. He sit down there looking so sad.

My eyes start to full up for him and because he was looking so lonely I give him a hug.

"You love your Pa, Sill?" He voice start to choke up when he ask me that. I nod against his chest and he squeeze me even tighter to him and start to play with my hair. The way we was sitting down, hugging was kind of awkward and he pull me on his lap, just like how he used to do when I was young and he used to tell me stories like *Snow White*.

"I love you too, Sill. You is the fairest of them all." And he continue to play with my hair and then he start to play with my leg and them. After a while he start to push he hand up under my skirt. Without knowing why I push he hands away.

"What happen? Why you do that? It have boys interfering with you in school?"

"No, Pa."

"So then how you know to push away my hands, eh?"

"Ma tell me not to let nobody touch me there, Pa."

"Well, I is your Pa. I different. I is not like them little boys in your school. Them will spoil you. I wouldn't spoil you. You is my princess."

And with that he start to tell me how much he love me. How since from the day I come home from the hospital I was he special girl. And how nothing nobody do could ever change how much he love me. While he saying all of this he hand moving higher and higher between my leg. Then he put he hand under my jersey and start to play up with my breasts and he was breathing hard and it wasn't feeling good. But I didn't want him to think I didn't love him so I just sit down quiet. Then I hear Ma voice and he push me off his lap and say, "It getting late, child. Let we go inside." He straighten out my clothes and while he doing it he say to me, "Now don't tell your Ma nothing, eh. She will get vex if she know I love you more than I love she. You have to promise me."

The way he say it, make me feel like we had a real special bond. Like we had we own secret from Ma. Something she couldn't touch. I feel I did understand Pa better.

"You can't tell nobody this, eh, Silla. They wouldn't understand how much I love you. You love your Pa plenty not so?"

"Yes, Pa."

"Right. Well not everybody does be happy when children love their parents like how you love me and how I love you. So you have to be quiet, eh. Because we ain't want to get nobody vex." And he watch the house like if he hearing the old talk in he head already, and I understand.

When we went back in the house Ma was still vex and she start to shout at me, "Where the hell you was all this time?"

Pa put she in she place one time. "The child was with me. You ain't fed up terrorise people in this house? If you quarrelling, quarrel with me but leave the child alone."

After that evening, once Ma quarrel with me, Pa used to put she in she place one time. It used to get she vex. But she didn't understand how close me and Pa was.

That shed become me and Pa own private world especially after he and Ma quarrel. Sometimes until real late in the night we would meet there and talk and thing. He tell me nobody can't come between us, ever. Now, sometimes when I meet Pa by the shop after school I don't go straight home. He does want to spend time with me there, before he have to go home and face the quarrel.

But it have something else I watching. I see him playing with Chandra hair this evening. The same way he used to be playing with mine in the beginning and Chandra done seeing she period and getting breast. If she feel she going and take Pa from me she lie. She done have Ma wrap round she finger already. I will do for she tail.

"Ma, look Chandra changing she clothes naked as she born and Rajin watching she!"

As soon as I say that Rajin with he cry-baby self go bawl out, "Ma is a lie. Silla lying on we."

★

Silla real wicked when she ready. She lie on we. Chandra wasn't naked. I didn't see nothing. I had my face in the pillow when Chandra was changing she clothes and the room was dark because it was almost night. In any case, Silla shouldn't talk about Chandra so. She stand up in the room watching me hard, hard. She feel I don't know that she don't like Chandra. Ma call Chandra in the kitchen. I feel she go get licks.

"What you and Chandra was talking about?"

"Nothing, Silla."

"You lie." And she pinch me. A hard pinch. My eyes start to full up and I feel myself getting vex. What Silla have to pinch me for. I didn't do she nothing.

"Tell me now. If you tell me, I will tell Ma it was a mistake and you wouldn't get no licks."

"I not telling you nothing. Because is you will get licks from Ma, not me."

Outside in the kitchen I hear Ma and Pa shouting and it sound like if Chandra getting licks.

"You see what you do? You see what you do? We wasn't doing nothing and you make Chandra get in trouble. I will tell Ma on you. I will tell Ma."

"Tell Ma what, you little ass? What it have for you to tell Ma?" And she pinch me again.

Same time the door open and I see Chandra walking in. I know if Silla pinch me again she will protect me.

"Pinch me again and you will see. Pinch me and I go tell everybody, everything."

"Tell what, you little fool? What you have to tell?"

And she start to walk up to me like she going to hit me so I bawl out, "If you only lash me I will tell Ma how I see you and Pa bulling behind the shop!"

Is only then I see Ma and Pa in the door behind Chandra.

BREAST POCKET

My first sexual relationship last seven years. We stop sexing when I turn fourteen because by that time plenty thing did happen in that house. People grow up and leave. People quarrel and leave and my mother and father did separate and Mammy wanted we to live with she and not by my father family. The judge and them in the courts side with she when she get the divorce and that did mean moving out from by Daddy. So without knowing it they kind of save me.

He was forty-five years older than me, but then I was so small I wasn't thinking bout that, so I didn't know his age. Is only now I start to check the age difference. It had all kinda reason why it happen and happen for so long. I used to think one reason was that nobody didn't know. He tell me point blank nobody go believe what I tell them because I black and does lie plenty; nobody does believe little black lying bitches. Because he skin red, he used to tell me all kinda thing, like how my skin so black and I should paint my skin white so that at least when we have outage he could see where my black ass hiding. If that was really the case I woulda wish for power outage all the time, because then he woulda never see me.

Everybody in the house did fraid him. Down to he wife, my aunt. When he reach home from work, all man used to get quiet. We ain't making a sound until he settle down and start to talk, because is only then everybody else feel they could talk. But even then we ain't talking loud. Not loud and jokey like when he wasn't there.

I didn't know for certain anything was wrong with how he touch me. Nobody ever talk bout them kind of thing, but I never used to feel good. I try to ask my aunt why he used to call my breast and them tomatoes, but she just shake she head and say, "Girl, what foolishness you talking?" I try plenty time to ask she thing, but from the time I bring up he name she used to either get quiet or talk bout something else.

And then my father wasn't there much in the house either. Most time he was offshore on a rig, and I didn't want to ask him nothing. We wasn't so close and I didn't know how to ask him thing bout my body. Then I did see a show on TV with a little girl who tell she mother some store-keeper was "touching she". The way she say it make it sound nice, much nicer than it does really feel. Because when that happening to you it don't feel like no touch. It does feel like if something nasty, real nasty like slimy swamp water all over you. You does feel like everybody watching you and know what you do and they seeing the nastiness on you. I try to tell Mammy, but she thought it was a joke, because she say "But everybody does touch people." Then not too long after that she and Daddy real fall out and she move to stay by she sister: a next auntie.

I hush-up after Mammy leave, because I remember how Uncle tell me nobody ain't go believe me. You must be wondering how I could think so. But picture yourself stretch out on a bed when you was small like me and this big man over you and he face set up vex because you trying to play smart and make a noise to get somebody, anybody attention and he come down close, close to your face and tell you, "Bitch, if you make a next sound I go damage you and nobody, nobody going to believe anything you say." You bound to be frighten.

After Mammy move out of the house it didn't really have anybody else I feel I could tell. Even though my aunt was real nice, real quiet and might have listened, I didn't want she to vex with me, especially since he was always vex with all a we.

Nobody ever say it wasn't suppose to happen. So I didn't know that your uncle wasn't supposed to do them things and get away with it. I think because he is the boss in the house, that is what I have to deal with, and I stay quiet. I sure my aunt have to deal with things and stay quiet too. Plenty time I see him cuss she up and threaten to hit she. All she do is stay quiet.

Sex wasn't something you was supposed to discuss. I feel he and my aunt never had sex, because they never had children. All I could say now is thank God my mother come and take we from them. I did fed up. Fed up feeling he hand on me. Fed up avoiding my aunt eyes when she come in a room and was me and he alone in it. But like it seem she never catch on. Them times, she never notice how loud and boisterous he get, calling she "darling" and "doux doux" and "Sweetheart". Them was the only times he ever call she them thing – while he hand wet from feeling me up.

Now this therapist woman want me to talk to my uncle. I tell she she is a mad ass. Week after week, she only riling me up to tell she things about my past. All kinda weird question about how I feel and what I think. Half the time I studying how I paying *she* to give me answers, not to ask me questions.

I doing this because two years after I get married, I stop being able to function with my husband. One minute I could do it and was enjoying it. Then one night he hand reach up and cup my breast and the next minute I feeling cold and sick. I looking down at he body under mine and I can't bear to touch him much less have him inside me. So just so I stop and roll off, and that was it. Weeks pass and we don't touch each other or talk bout what happen. I think my husband feel was he fault. He feel he was the one that turn me off.

One day he walk in the bathroom and catch me watching myself in the mirror, cupping my breast. That was the straw to break the camel back.

"You fucking somebody else?"

I stop and take my time turning off the shower. "What you think?"

"Well, why we not doing it?"

"Because I ain't have no feelings. I tell you that already."

"So you ain't have feelings for me but you have feelings for yourself? That is what you saying? I just see you touching yourself. You expect me to believe you just turn off me just so? You don't even let me touch you no more. When last I even get to see you naked?"

"Yesterday morning. I was bathing and you come in to brush your teeth." I shouldn't have answer him so. The way I was talking was hurting him, but it was that or let him see the hurt in me.

He eye did full up when he leave for work that morning. He wanted to say something to kill the awkwardness between us. I did feel it too but I stay quiet. After he leave I sit down and try to cry, but all I do is retch in the face basin a little.

Is not that Lance didn't know something happen between me and my uncle. I just never give details. I didn't think after all this time pass it woulda start to bother me. Years now me ain't study it and then memories just come back with that one thing. That hand on my breast.

I couldn't bring myself to tell him about why I was cupping my breast. I couldn't tell him that all them years ago that was the signal. I would be in the kitchen washing wares or in the bedroom putting away clothes and he would just come up behind me and put he hand on one of my breast and that was the signal. I had no choice. Is lie down and take it. Now, whenever Lance touch my breast, especially from behind, I want to vomit and pull off my skin. This body and brain so treacherous.

He come home that evening real subdue and ask me to go out to dinner with him. I know what he was trying. When we did first meet and was courting, he did do the same thing. I used to tease him and ask him what a boy from Rousillac know about candlelight dinner, and who flower garden he thiefing all them bouquet from? He was a man like to feel he romantic and thing. Any little problem between we and he go do something to try to patch thing up. He does still try to surprise me with a little gift and thing, "To keep the love fresh," he say.

I agree to go with him but my heart wasn't in it. Flowers and wine and sweet talk wasn't going to change things and when it fail, I know he go feel like an ass, or worse, start to hate me. In the middle of eating, while I waiting for the sweet talk, he ask me to see a therapist. He hit me for six with that one. We is not people like that, just go and talk we business with strangers. I know for he to ask me to do this take plenty nerve, because how he go feel for me to tell a perfect stranger that I don't feel for him, and he can't excite me? But I say yes, because I know for him to do this was a big thing, and if I didn't make a try the same way he making a try, and things didn't work out, he go hate me. I didn't want that.

From the get go I know was a mistake. The woman want to know everything. Relative I forget about, she ask about. Things I didn't even realize I do, people I didn't realize I hate, she force me to remember. The whole time I opening up myself she only hmmmming and scribbling on a yellow notepad. She fee and them was good high too. I tell Lance I sure she putting in a spa or a jacuzzi in she house from my sessions alone.

It was only after the fourth or fifth time I see she that I decide was worth it to stay. She ask me about my mother and when I start to give details, the tears come. I never cry like that before. It seemed to come from my toes and shoot up into my stomach. The tears didn't feel like water, it was like a lava flow, hot, thick. I must be cry for a good forty-five minutes of the fifty-five I did get in every session. In between the tears I trying to explain, but I just couldn't. My nose running snot and whole time I only saying, "Oh God" and, "I stopping now". That day was a turning point.

In the weeks that follow I explain about my mother. How before I move out to live with my birth mother, my aunt did come like my mother when I was living by she. Is something I did never tell anybody or even realize for myself. After Mammy leave, even when Mammy was there, this aunt did come like a next mother. I did trust she.

"Them was weak bitches! She especially!" I burst out one evening.

"Uhhmmmmmm… weak how?"

"Them… She… she never stand up to him. She take one set of shit from him and leave we to take shit from him too!"

"Uhmmmmmm. Who is 'him'?" Scribble, scribble, scribble.

"You not listening. If you was listening you wouldn't ask all them dotish question. You think what she do was right, eh? You always asking question, well listen to me and answer one of mine! You think it right that all them adults was around and we children had was to face that! If he ain't vex and cutting we ass, he have me in a corner in some room! You ain't answering?"

"I am listening… I want to hear you say his name. You never say his name. You avoid saying it by using something else – or by snapping at me."

"He name 'Uncle'." I wanted to provoke she. To make she lose control the way I feel I was losing mine. But them thing don't work with she. I feel to be a therapist you can't have any feelings. I wonder how she husband does make out with she – if she does ever feel anything. And because I was vex I ask she that too. But she ain't take me on.

"Does this uncle have a name?" More blasted scribbling.

I sit down for a while watching she, but my mind studying more than it watching. This woman *know* what it taking from me to call the bitch name? She ain't even know what it take to talk about any of them thing. To explain about how use up I feel. To talk about a sexual relationship that wasn't really a relationship, but at the same time my body and my mind was involved, so was still a relationship. How to explain to this cross-to-bear in front of me that even though I didn't like what was going on, it had times I was willing to sex with him because it mean he go be in a better mood and no licks for we in the house? How to explain that in calling he name I might bring all of him back? All the memories – including the ones in the deepest, darkest corners. Because is not one or two thing I do with him. Is all. It have thing if I think about it too long I might vomit. Even she might vomit.

I get up to leave.

"You still have thirty minutes. You want to use them or add them to your next session?"

She ain't even look up when she talking. I was hurting. I wanted to bawl until my voice go and my throat so raw I could focus on *that* pain instead of the one in my chest. But I decide to try it.

"He name Richard."

"I think you should meet with him. Tell him how you feel. In exactly the words you used here today. Get it off your chest. More than one person needed to stand up to him, obviously. While you're angry with all of them, there is only one person you're really blaming, hmmmmm? And there is at least one person you need to confront."

After that session I decide I wasn't taking she on. The man dead. How I go confront him? I tell she I only interested in couple's counselling after that. Because I know if I didn't make myself clear she would keep on my case. How could I go see him and get things off my chest? And even if Uncle was alive, is everyday you does walk up to a man and ask him why he interfere with you when you was still a child? Like it would be easy to admit to this man that he spoil me for every man after him, even the husband whom I love, the same husband who I thought would have been able to chase away the demons and them that does be in my head. And Uncle dead.

But it had a day. We was standing up in the line in the grocery and I see a couple walk in. The man resemble my uncle. The woman didn't look nothing like my aunt, but she have the same kind of behaviour – quiet, patient. He was roughing she up in the grocery. The same way Uncle used to rough up my aunt when the mood take him. Lance ain't say nothing. He stand up quiet in the line and watch me watch them. He didn't sound surprise that night when I tell him what I wanted to do.

So that is why me and Lance stand up in Rousillac cemetery like two fool. He start to walk round pretending to look at the different graves to give me space. I stand up a good while before I say anything. The first thing I try was: "You was a worthless son of a bitch." But it sound weak and stupid. The cow and goat grazing close by ain't even look up at me.

"Maybe if I say prick", I think. I did learn that word from him. He used to tell me, "Don't tell nobody that I put my prick in you, eh." But it ain't sound right either. It sound empty… This wasn't going to work – this stand up in a field talking to cow and goat.

Lance find me sitting on the mound of dirt. He stop, like he did fraid. Unsure how I would take his closeness.

"So what you tell him?"

"That he was a prick."

"How he take it?"

"Oh… He just lie down and ain't say a word."

"How you feel?" He was smiling now because at least I was making jokes.

I stand up to dust off my skirt, clear my throat and put on my best town accent. "Like a sexually abused young woman who's trying to make sense of her life and save her marriage."

"You sound fancy like the therapist. What you want to do now?"

I look at him for a while and turn away saying nothing. I feel rather than hear his move toward me. I slacken my hands at my side to allow him to hold me. He was real careful. Not once he hand even brush my breast, and that move me, because it mean he did remember. But is when I feel the perspiration from he face on the back of my neck I make my decision. Uncle wasn't winning again today or any other time. I take Lance hand and put it inside my shirt to hold me there.

"Something wrong with the food?" Shirley's words shook Ralph out of his contemplation of the plate of ochroes, saltfish and rice cook-up in front of him. He wasn't really hungry, but figured if he didn't eat, it would spoil his wife's seeming good mood.

"No…," he cleared his throat, "I was just thinking."

"You want something to drink? Juice? Coconut water?"

"It have coconut water?"

She poured out a glass and left the half-full bottle on the table in case he wanted a refill and headed back to the living room. At the doorway, she hesitated, eyes darting from him to the dirty pots in the kitchen sink. Ralph thought she wanted to say something. His stomach started to clench up again, waiting for the storm to break. He swallowed a forkful of rice to show her he had started eating and needed some peace. Surprisingly, he felt his taste buds spring to life and his appetite open up. But by the time he looked up to compliment her on the food, Shirley had left him to his meal.

Strange. How come Shirley was in a good mood this evening? A damn good mood. It quite threw him off balance. He had spent the drive home from work bracing himself for another storm, with Shirley cussing and carrying on and hurling accusations left, right and centre. She would fly at him as soon as he was through the door. Just recently, it seemed the only kind of behaviour she was capable of.

But this evening, she'd been sitting in front of the television looking at something about home improvement. She announced quietly that the children were over at their aunt's house visiting. He'd been so grateful for the reprieve that he'd actually smiled at her and she'd smiled back. He wanted to talk to her, and he didn't want the children present, to witness Shirley flying off the handle.

What the hell going on here, boy? Her face looked different too, more guarded. Was this the quiet before the storm?

Back in the living room Shirley died a thousand deaths. She wanted to stay in the dining room and make sure that Ralph ate every last grain of the ochro rice. She figured he was still angry with her after how she had behaved that morning. She didn't give him wrong. If the situation was reversed, she would have been angry with her too. She had cussed him all the way out of the house, precisely the thing she had promised herself she wouldn't do. Afterwards she was so pissed off with herself that she collapsed on the living room couch crying, until her friend Agnes came at 10 o'clock and forced her to clean herself up. She had forgotten they were going out.

In the car she had started up her usual litany.

"Why, Agnes? Eh? Why?"

Agnes continued to stare hard at the road, just resisting the urge to blow out Shirley herself. As much as she understood what Shirley was going through, she was fed up with the self-pity party. It had been six months since Shirley found out about Ralph's philandering.

"You remember when you met Ralph?"

Shirley nodded. "I could ever forget that? He ignore me the whole time. He was so full of himself. Remember, is that other girl… What was her name? Karen, yes, Karen Rodriguez… that he was sweet on. But he couldn't get through with she and eventually we started going out."

"You ever thought then you was going to marry him."

"Girl, I know from the minute I meet Ralph we was going to get married. Is he that didn't know it."

"You regret it now?"

Shirley remained silent for a while. "No. If I was to meet him again I would still get married to him."

"Even though he horn you? Girl, what you go do about it? You can't just sit there sniffing."

Shirley said nothing, and continued to sniff. She was remembering the confrontation when she had found out.

"You damn worthless bitch!" she had screamed at him, "Fifteen years and two children. You have no respect for yourself. Or for me!"

The relationship was almost a year old. The girl was, as expected, considerably younger – and in Shirley's mind probably more sophisticated and intelligent than she was.

To Agnes' mind, the problem was that instead of making a choice between leaving Ralph's cheating ass or fighting to keep him, Shirley had just fallen into a deep depression, put on disgusting amounts of weight and walked around with a long long face. Perhaps Shirley thought that if Ralph saw how depressed she was, it would prompt him to do the right thing. It didn't.

As far as Agnes could tell, it was only when Shirley's face got long enough and her bottom had achieved a dangerous state of wideness that she started fighting with Ralph, pointing out his faults and picking arguments with him over the smallest things, but never giving him an ultimatum. Perhaps Shirley was too afraid to address the real issue. Afraid that if they actually sat down and talked about Ralph's affair, she might hear things that she wasn't ready for. But the constant cursing was evidently water off a duck's back, because Ralph did nothing and Shirley was just getting more sour with life. But Agnes had said all these things to Shirley several times. There was no point in repeating them. It was time for action.

There were things that Shirley had not told Agnes, such as the day *Oprah* inspired her to try reverse psychology on Ralph and become the sexy, enigmatic person she imagined Ralph wanted her to be. She would put some spice back into their marriage and try some of the antics that guests on the show guaranteed would work. Shirley felt certain that *the girl* had used those tricks, or similar, to lure Ralph. She started cajoling, petting, cooking his favourite meals and experimenting with make-up. But the gestures only irritated him. She even tried to entice him by rolling herself in Saran wrap from neck to toe one night and draping herself decoratively on the bed. When Ralph stepped into their bedroom, panic showed on his face.

"You should leave the cold cuts in the fridge," he said, and turned and went into the bathroom.

In the long night hours she wondered what had gone wrong. Had she become too complacent? Was she too clingy or dependent on him? Wasn't she supposed to be that way? Did Ralph now want an independent, career woman? She remembered how before their marriage his mother had pulled her aside and told her plainly, "Ralph not looking for no modern woman who working and ain't have time to look after a husband and a house you know." Then, she had felt that Ralph's mother had been envious that she was at university and had the chance to make something of herself. She had smiled politely at the advice. But later, when they were attending a wedding, Ralph had said to one of his friends, "Boy I don't know how he going and make out with that one he get married to. When he wake up after the honeymoon and realize he have to cook, wash and clean for heself, I hope he still having and holding and cherishing until death do them part." Shirley concluded there were compromises she would have to make.

It was easy at first. She had the man she wanted and a baby was on the way. It was almost like playing house. He would go off to work and she would cook, clean and prepare for his return. She had to admit that she had never really got fed up with this routine while the children were still young. They had both seemed happy.

She'd even tried using the children to make sure that he could see how much they needed him at home. Without actually mentioning the D word, she began mobilising them to spend more "quality time" with their father – as Oprah and Doctor Phil were always recommending. Families on the show cried and hugged a lot, pending divorces were postponed and all the couples were vowing to "work things out." Soon Regina and Richard were regularly calling on Ralph for games of Scrabble, and giving voice to Shirley's suggestions for family outings at the weekends.

Ralph had drawn the line when, on Shirley's prompting, they began asking him whether he loved them or not. The first time he had looked around, panicked and confused. He had caught Shirley's searching gaze. Regina had asked the question.

"Yes, darling, of course," he stammered. "Daddy will always love you." He didn't have to tell the children he loved them. He just did. But Regina had pressed on.

"Mommy too?"

He had grunted, angry to have been forced into that situation.

The next time the question came up, Ralph was ready with an answer.

"Reggie, honey…" Ralph shot a glance sideways at Shirley, "I don't know where this is coming from, but my feelings for your mother are at a level they have never been before."

The words had sent a chill through Shirley. A divorce was looming. She was sure of it. The sonofabitch intended to cheat her out of what was rightfully hers. It wouldn't surprise her if he'd already talked to some damned lawyer and papers were being drawn up. She would be left to pick up the pieces of her's and her children's lives.

She knew that Ralph had always resented the speed with which they had married, though even he thought they had done the right thing. She couldn't be pregnant and unwed; it simply would not do. Both of their families would have been horrified, though both their mothers had suspected instantly, their eyes flying to Shirley's stomach.

"This is what I sacrifice for?" Shirley's mother accused. "I thought after the way you see your mother struggle, you woulda do something with the opportunity you get. Now you planning to be a housewife?"

Shirley had come from a farming family in Princes Town, and while they weren't dirt poor, they weren't wealthy either. Shirley's mother had never had the chance to become a "modern woman" as she called girls of Shirley's age and she hoped Shirley would become. This marriage was a regressive step. Shirley tried to console her.

"But Ma, he will look after me. I wouldn't have to work."

"I rather you work than stay home to mind a man and

child. How pregnant you is? You sure you want to have this child?"

"Ma! What you saying?" Shirley exclaimed.

"Now is not like my time, Shirley. All you young people could choose all you husband and make love match now. All you could wait longer to get married. You feel is now they invent abortion? Plenty woman throw away child in my time to save theirself. You could make a next one."

Shirley had been stunned by the sadness on her mother's face. She hadn't realized the news would have disappointed her mother so much.

As he told Shirley, Ralph, too, had his share of family disappointment to deal with.

"We wasn't expecting this," his mother had said. "We say you woulda get a job and after a little while settle down with a girl who working in a bank or teaching or something. We say you woulda establish yourself a little before you do this thing."

And the truth was, Ralph had felt resentful. He wanted more. He couldn't quite say what that was, but knew this was not it. But their parents all agreed that since there was a child on the way, the right thing, in spite of their disappointment, would have to be done.

But Ralph's resentment had lessened when Regina was born and with two children, their own home, a good job and a comfortable life, Shirley would have said that Ralph seemed contented with his lot and with the life they had created. She hadn't seen the horn coming.

The first seed of doubt had been planted one evening she was watching "Lifetime Television" with Agnes. Ralph was having another late night at the office. The movie was about some woman who was giving so much attention to her autistic child that she'd ignored her husband, who had then had an affair. Agnes had looked at her and asked, "You think that might be happening to you?"

"I would notice if the children were autistic, Agnes!"

Agnes rolled her eyes. "Nah girl. I doubt it. Ralph know where he bread butter. He getting everything he need right here."

Shirley had laughed that night, but she began to monitor his behaviour when he continued the frequent late nights at the office. Sometimes, when she called she got him. Other times, he had stepped out to the photocopier or fax machine and hadn't heard the phone or checked its messages. There was also a noticeable chill in the bedroom.

One night it took him almost two hours to photocopy a document and return her call. She hired a private investigator. A week later she knew everything she needed to know about the young and exciting Ms Welch – address, occupation, home, mobile and office phone numbers, favourite foods, etcetera. She had half-dozen pictures of an attractive, well-proportioned brown-skinned woman with shoulder-length hair cavorting at the beach with Ralph. He could hardly have looked happier.

Agnes pulled up in a lay-by. This was no use. It was driving her crazy to listen to Shirley sniffing beside her.

"Girl, you real let yourself go in these last few months. All you studying is this man and the blasted woman and like you forget it had Shirley involved in this too. You so gone you ain't even taking on the children. Everyday they by their aunt or me."

Agnes' tone hurt.

"You think it easy eh, Agnes? You feel it easy for me to watch you with your career and your freedom and watch how organized you is all the time? You feel it easy to listen to you talk about the challenges of your job while all I could talk 'bout is the new set of curtains I buy in Queensway or the fridge I eyeing in Courts? You think a time didn't come when I get fed up of being this? Eh?"

"I know you fed up long time. But what you doing about it? You is a woman could hold down a whole house and in two days transform it, yet you telling me these last few months you don't know what to do. Look, girl, you have to do something. Let me visit a woman I know who could fix he up good!"

Agnes' mother was a Tobagonian who believed most things could be solved by a good bush bath or a spirit lash. She credited her own success to the many bush baths she had taken as a child.

"Why?" Shirley had asked between tears.

"So he ass could shrivel up and dead nah. I fed up sit down and watch you cry. I fed up get phone calls during the day and all you doing on the other end is crying and asking me the same damn questions and threatening to go and kill the woman. I fed up of you sitting beside me sniffing! I think if you put a good spirit lash on him everybody problem solved."

"No, Agnes, I love him. That is my husband. I don't want nobody else."

"So you feel the best thing to do is to continue to suffer and accept his shit? You even realize the position you in right now? You make a child for this man straight out of university. That degree ain't get used yet because you stay home for the last fifteen years raising children. You have no job. When… yes when… he decide to leave your ass, what you planning to do? Live off alimony?"

"No, Agnes. I understand what you saying but you don't understand how hard this is. I don't know anything else but life with Ralph. I can't just turn my back on him… on this just so."

Agnes looked unconvinced.

"You joking about the obeah right?"

Agnes smiled.

Shirley didn't know what she was expecting, something spooky maybe, but not the woman in front of her. She looked like a business executive on holiday, though what, exactly, were obeah women supposed to look like? Old, fat, smelly, head wrapped in colourful scarves and wearing clothes with loud clashing colours?

"So, yes," said the executive obeah woman, "how can I help you?"

There was an uncomfortable silence. Agnes said, "Well, we seem to have a bit of a problem where…"

"My husband horning me and I want to kill his ass!"

Both Agnes and the obeah woman stared at Shirley.

"Okay, maybe not kill. But I… I want to keep him, but I want him to suffer a little bit… and I want him to stay. I want him to stay."

"Define suffer," the obeah woman said.

"I want him to feel sorry that he played the ass. I want him to realize that I is a good wife."

"So not physical suffering? Well, he will only feel remorse when he is truly sorry and then his conscience will prick him more than I can. So I can't help with that. But I can do something else."

Shirley leaned forward, eyes wide open, her voice barely a whisper, "Like what?"

Later that evening, when she walked into the kitchen and looked at the iron pot in the sink, she couldn't help chuckling as she remembered her antics earlier that day. She had been appalled at first by what the obeah woman had suggested.

"Sweat rice? A pot of rice will keep him?"

"It's not just normal rice," she had assured her. "This rice will have your essence in it. He will not be able to get you out of his system."

Agnes had helped her to climb onto the counter. With her right leg on the counter, her left leg on the far side of the stove, Shirley straddled the pot of rice that was bubbling away. She allowed the steam from the pot to lick its way up her legs, past her thighs into the higher regions under her skirt. She winced as the steam from the boiling pot of rice condensed and made its way back to the pot.

Shirley had been sceptical. But the promise that Ralph would be unable to get over her made it seem worth trying. That and Agnes. While she teetered over the pot and complained about the pain, Agnes kept her steady and made ridiculous jokes about steamed saltfish and boiled saltfish. Agnes really was a fool. Shirley didn't know why she thought her sophisticated at all. She had said this and Agnes had laughed.

"Just think you giving yourself a spa treatment, girl. Ent that is what Oprah does advise you to do."

Shirley was still chuckling as she remembered this comment that she didn't hear Ralph come in. She jumped when she realized that he was standing in the doorway behind her, holding his empty plate.

"What so funny?"

She considered him for a minute. "Life."

"Life have you killing yourself with laugh so?"

"Yes, boy, life."

Ralph shook his head and started leaving the kitchen.

"Ralph…"

He paused and turned. It would start now. He felt it.

"Look, I know you have this woman. I know things not so good between us right now. I know we quarrelling plenty right now." She paused as she saw him flinch.

"I know that I get on like a real ass in the last few months. But you help out, too. So it have a few things I want you to know. Things have to change around here. I not telling you what to do about this woman. But I going to look for a job and start to see about me. I not letting you take me for granted anymore. It have more to me than minding this house and you and the children and cooking meals whole day." She ran out of breath as she noticed how Ralph was looking at her.

"Why you watching me so funny? Ahhh… you waiting for me to cuss you? Sorry, Ralph. I fed up being vex with you and vex with me. It have more for me to do with myself than to be vex and sorry for myself all the time."

Shirley turned back to the sink and continued to wash the dishes. She felt him standing there, staring at her back. She felt him step forward and kept herself still, all the time rinsing and washing.

He was wondering if this was the time to let her know that he, too, had come to a decision, that the marriage and their family meant more to him than the girl. He wanted to tell her that it wasn't going to be easy, but that he was willing to try. But he was afraid to spoil the tranquillity of the moment. Shirley seemed so calm. He didn't want another argument. Especially after what she had just said.

He cleared his throat awkwardly.

"The food taste good."

She looked at him and smiled. "I know. I cook it especially for you."

The conversation was not going well.

"Why can't you leave her?"

"I didn't say I couldn't. I just don't think I should do it this way."

"What way? You're not making sense." She felt her eyes beginning to fill and willed them not to. She took a deep breath to control the tremor she felt entering her voice. She clasped her hands behind her back and allowed the nails to bite into her skin.

"I'll ask again, even though I know I'll get the same response. Do you love me?"

"You know I do."

"Do you love her?"

"No, I don't. But I don't hate her either. She has her good points."

"What is your fucking obsession with good points? Do you love me because of good points?"

He sighed. Her anger paralysed him. He just didn't know what to say when she was in a mood like this.

"Jenny, I need more time."

"More time! More time!" Her voice rose to a near shriek. "More time for what? I've given you a year! You asked me for three months to sort out your shit and I've given you a year. A year of understanding. A year of patience. A year of unfuckingbelieveable pain and suffering and now you ask for more time!"

.She sounded on the edge of hysteria and he wondered how much longer before she started crying. He was dying to check his watch but knew how she would interpret that. He just needed to get her calmer, laughing a bit, maybe even crying a bit, but not this hysterical anger.

"I know I'm being unreasonable, Jenny, but please bear with me. Hear me out. I don't want things to end bitterly."

"But what about us? Suppose we end bitterly? Don't you care that this could end us?"

"Jenny, of course, I care. I don't want us to end…"

"But you don't want you and her to end either, do you?" It was the same goddamned circle every time. She would beg and plead. He would promise to end things… eventually. Then the weeks would pass, the months would pass and still nothing.

"You're a coward, you know that!"

"Jenny, how would *you* feel if I broke up with you just like that?" He snapped his finger to emphasise his point. "No explanations, no reasons, nothing."

"Well, try it now. Let's see?"

This was becoming dangerous. He didn't want to push her to any rash decisions. He might not want this conversation, but he still wanted her. The last time she'd got so angry, she'd gone to Sabrina's office to force a confrontation. He had only worked his way out of that with great difficulty. It had taken months of cajoling on either side.

"Jenny," his voice took on a softer, pleading tone, "just give me some more time. I'm close to putting an end to this thing. I just need a few more months. She's bound to screw up. She knows that she gets on my nerves. I'm only doing this to make things absolutely certain…"

"Certain of what? You're still uncertain? It's been three years, Stephen. What are you still uncertain of, me or you?"

"Look, Jen," he took her hand in his, "I need to keep things balanced, until I leave."

"When are you leaving?"

"I said soon."

"Give me a time frame. Soon can mean anything, coming from you."

"I'm not sure."

"Are you ready to leave her?"

"I… yes." Her face was changing again. It had started off as such a peaceful afternoon. The sex had been pleasurable. They had slept and when he awoke she had been working away quietly at her computer. He had turned on the television for lack of something to do and she had abandoned her work to come watch it with him. It was the damn movie that had triggered things off.

"You're lying. Stop lying. Tell me the truth. If you don't want to end things with her, just tell me." Her voice was filled with anguish now.

"Tell me the fucking truth and I'll deal with it. I'll move on." She was lying, they both knew it. She had threatened this before and had made a half-hearted attempt at leaving, but his pleas had kept her.

"Jenny, stop it! Just stop it."

"End it!"

"No!"

"Why not? Why not, you prick!? How many more months this time? How much more of this do you think I can take?"

His tone was measured, "I promise I'll work things…"

"You're a liar. You're not doing anything. You're waiting on one of us to end things for you. That's the only way

104

you'll make a choice; when we force one on you. I could be with other men, you know." She had flung that at him in the past and he knew then it was true, but he also knew she didn't have the taste for it anymore. The time for her to move on had long since passed.

"Look, this is going nowhere. Let's just calm down and try to enjoy the rest of the evening together." He knew that was impossible and wondered what time it was. He didn't want to miss dinner. There would be hell to pay if he couldn't explain his absence.

"Tell me why you won't leave her. Tell me now. Tell me or I'll hurt one of us!" He tried to read her expression. She just might. She had tried it in the past. Lost total control of herself to bring him to her side.

"It's just not a good time, Jenny. Give me a few months."

"Why months? Why not weeks?"

"Jenny."

"Stephen, I want an answer. A good, sound, comprehensive answer. You don't give me one and we're both going to end up in a hospital tonight."

From the look on her face he thought she meant it.

"Sabrina's…" He stopped. There was no way out. There would be histrionics whether or not he told her.

"Sabrina's what?" She was sneering now.

"Pregnant." The words landed with a thud between them. Jenny wrapped a hand around her middle, awkwardly trying to hug herself. Inside her head she said, Don't fall, don't fall.

"If you just give me a few months. After the baby is born it will all…"

"Go home, Stephen." Her voice was quiet.

It was the release he had been waiting for. He made an attempt to hug her, but she was still hugging herself and that made it awkward. She kept perfectly still. He shut the door quietly behind him. She waited until his car was a distant noise and walked to the bathroom. Off the highest shelf she took down the used applicator and stared at it. She had planned to tell him tonight. They would have made love again, laughed and made plans around it, if that damned movie hadn't set her off. It was what he'd always wanted, or so he said.

Two pink lines on the pregnancy test mocked her.

GAPS

It was one of those lazy Saturdays that was normally Me Time on Maracas beach with my Kindle. Instead, I carry Nicole up to the coast with me. She's good fun. Great sense of humour and knows when to talk and when to hush. I was sprawled out, flat on my back, letting the sun darken my stomach, searching thought my digital library for another book to read.

"Look at that child there."

"Where?"

"By the edge of the water. Playing with the bucket and shovel by himself. He gorgeous. Nice mix."

I push myself up on my elbows to see this child.

"Yeah. Nice mix."

"I wouldn't mind making one so, you know. But I don't really want the hassle of an Indian boyfriend."

"So the boyfriend would be a hassle, but not the child?"

"If the father willing to give me a child and go he road, then I good. I could see myself with a nice dougla child. But not necessarily with the father."

We went quiet for a while, watching the child play. His mother was a few yards away, keeping an eye on him making sand pies that kept getting washed away.

"I had an Indian boyfriend once. I think," I say.

"What? What you mean you think? Is either you had one or you didn't."

"Is a kinda weird story."

"How long all yuh was together?"

"I don't know. Maybe a week, maybe a decade?"

"Now you talking in riddles. Maybe you should start at the beginning."

"Actually, I think I go start at the end…"

I drift off a bit after that, and is Nicole fidgeting that prompt me to start.

"Girl, what to say? How to start?"

"It was the sort of meeting only a fete could make possible. A jumble of people around. Bodies press up, hands in the air, drinks waving about as everyone shouting, "Feting is we name, we don't play, We going night and day…" A hand snake around my waist and I look to see who was tiefing a wine. Nobody from my crew. He look like a stranger but was grinning so triumphantly. Familiar, yuh know? Gradually the features fall into place.

Good Lord, Janak? I say.

I start to smile, then almost stop, wondering about my make-up, my fat belly, whether my clothes looking good.

He grin wider and wine harder, hands gripping my hips like only two old firesticks from a lost era could grip on each other. I cock back and grind too.

I remember the last time we cross paths. The sour note we did end on. So, I was happy that the fete don't allow too much words. We laugh. Exhilarated and self-conscious at the same time. He tell me he was there feting with some partners from work, who were wining protectively around a cooler.

He wanted to know who my crew was, whether I had a man, whether anyone would mind if he took two, three more wine with me.

I tell him I was there with my friends just liking myself. No stress, no worries. I make it clear that I was glad to see him.

We didn't end up in bed that night. But I wanted to, eh. No lie. I wanted to know if I'd missed out on something by turning him down. But between the two of us things was always complicated.

I grow up with J. All that separate we for years was a stretch of pitch. He was literally the boy next door. Or, across the road. Before I even know the names for genitals, me and he did know what one another other private parts look like, you know? We grow up that close. Bathing together as children. Sharing in the rituals of each other's households. Back and forth between both we yards every day.

He older, by three years if I remember right. So he enter primary school before me. Did Secondary Entrance exams before me and start work before me. But life funny, eh. As a child, your parents does keep things from you. They let you play with everybody. Let you think that everybody is the same. Everybody equal. Then as you get bigger things change. J went Junior Sec. When he pass his Secondary Exams, I didn't understand that him not passing for the Catholic boy's school was a big deal. He seem happy, and I happy for him. Then came my turn. Is around then things start to shift. Less playtime outside. More studying and drilling. Honestly, that exam was the hardest thing I ever do. Then I pass. I pass for the Catholic girl's school. It was in the papers. The whole village did know. His parents were one of the first to call across the road and congratulate me. Mammy, his mother – everybody call her Mammy – send over dhalpuri roti and curry goat as a congratulations. He bring it himself and we sit down in the gallery and talk about me passing for big school. I was excited. I pass and pass well. That day self he did tell me I would change. I didn't take him on. He tell me I was brighter than him and wouldn't find time for a duncy boy like him no more. Which was a joke. He was fourteen, I was eleven. He already had girlfriends. I couldn't even make a miss and think about boys. My house was real strict about those things. I had a father, mother, uncle, aunt, cousins and a whole street monitoring my movements. He know that.

But what change us wasn't school; it was the divorce. When my parents split up, he and I split up too. I move. We didn't see each other too often, and only for brief periods. The weekends my father had custody we spend mostly outdoors and in drives and excursions. The time me and J spend together was comfortable but brief. We use to stand up and talk on each other's front gap. Talk about tests, subjects, studies, TV shows, music. We both love Kasey Kasem and Rick Dees. Bon Jovi was our favourite band. We made chow together, with mangoes from his yard and chadon beni from mine. I spend every Divali by his home, helping to clean up and light deya. For Christmas and New Year's he would always come over the road and spend a few hours with us, liming, watching a movie or playing a hand of rummy.

Despite all we had in common, he had this idea that my world was real stush, real elite, you know. All girls. Catholic. Seven straight years at one school doing two sets of exams, while his education get break up between two schools over five years. He did a trade in his fourth and fifth year. Plumbing. I did subjects that required lab books and experiments. That intrigue him. Then, when I was eighteen, Mammy died. Though we know she had a weak heart, her death surprised us. Mummy allowed me to spend that weekend, a non-custody weekend, she pointed out, with my father so that I could be at the cremation.

It was just like childhood all over again. I spend all day in and out of his house. Helping with the cleaning and tidying up for the wake. I help my aunt and them bake sweetbread and brew coffee and pass them around. J bring the nuts, cracked and husked; I grate and mix ingredients. I wipe chairs; he set them out. We side by side all weekend long.

Daddy drive him and me to the cremation. J's father's car was filled with other siblings and relatives. He hold my hand that whole car ride. Grip it hard. It thrill me. No lie. At the cremation site I stand with my family, looking on at Mammy's last rites, familiar, yes, but still foreign, because the language, songs, prayers and rituals were not mine. They belong to J's world. He stand with his family but keep looking over to where I stood, smiling slightly at times. And I was smiling back. When it was time to light the pyre, I walk over to where he standing and hug him. He cry on my shoulder that day. When the pundit tell his relatives to light up Mammy's pyre, I try to step aside to let him do his part, but he hold my hand. Refuse to let go. So I stay by his side.

Daddy is not a man big on arguments or confrontation, eh. That evening as he drive me back to my mother house his comment was brief. He know J is my friend. But he tell me I have to be careful with the messages I sending. I knew what he mean. I didn't bother to play coy. So all I said to him was, yes.

Months pass before anything else happen. Not that we didn't see one another. We did, on weekends. Things went back to casual conversations. At least on the surface. But now every glance, touch or word seemed charged. J began commenting on my appearance and clothing. That was new. He would check around before making his comments. Say things like, nice shorts, today, or, no bra, eh? You trying to give men heart attack? I would flirt back, then feel guilty the moment I see my father watching us.

Then exams came and weekends were taken up with studying. I didn't see J for months. Not until July. Then exams were over and I could breathe. All I was interested in was liming with my friends. Beaches, cinemas, house limes, parties. It felt so good. Daddy promise me and my friends a trip down the islands, to go see the Gasparee caves. It was the first weekend in months I spent in Cunupia. When I saw J that Friday evening, he was still being pleasant. Came over to say hello and ask how exams went. But he was quieter. Laughing less, staring at me seriously as I talk about the various exams and tell him about the trip to Gasparee Island

Then he ask what I was doing that Sunday, and I say nothing, and we fence around a bit until I agree to come with him to a matinee cinema show.

I wait until we're on Gasparee Island and Daddy's distracted by my friends to mention this date, which I try to make sound not like a date, like it's normal for J to ask me to go out to the cinema. I pass it off as an I-survived-my-exams lime that J's gifting me. Only, the lime have just two people.

I could see Daddy weighing and gauging in his head. Ok, he say, for the 4:30 show, so I push my luck, say we might go for pizza afterwards. Back by eleven he says, all severe. Eleven was reasonable. I'd expected a no. I was giddy with triumph.

I don't know *what* the movie was about. Some action film with Steven Segal or that Van Damme fella. They were the hot action stars back then. I *can* tell you how J taste and how I feel, that I want him to touch me and that I touch him back – as much as bucket seats allow. We leave the movie early and walk around the backstreets of Chaguanas. Talking. Him saying just how long he's wanted me, had felt different about me. The funeral, I tell him. Since the funeral. Even before that, he says. But the funeral, with me helping out and being there through his pain make up his mind. We can't stop kissing and touching that evening, but we had to. In the taxi we hold hands, I lean against him. We couldn't hold hands in the street, but our bodies brush against each other, at the shoulders, or fingers. At my gap he whisper urgently, So, next week? And I whisper back, Yes. Then he say louder, maybe a little too loud. It sound like a guilty loud to me. The film was good, girl. We must lime again.

Daddy's waiting inside, pretending to watch TV. Before I even say hello he tells me I can't date that boy. I protest. We not dating. He's a friend. Fear and guilt grip me. But he says he's not stupid. He can see what starting and I must not become involved with that boy. He tells me J might think he likes me, but he's sure J hasn't informed his father about his feelings for me. We can be friends. Nothing else.

When I ask why, he says it's because we come from different worlds. Different worlds? He grow up here, I grow up here. Different how?

Then he gets annoying in that father way. You not going to understand this now, he says. When the time comes for you to have friends, have friends that are like you, Rachel. Then he comes out with it: have friends that are mixed. I ask him what's wrong with me having an Indian boyfriend. Nothing, he says, but that I'll be treated differently by his family and he doesn't want me made to feel different or inferior to anybody. He says J's family won't accept me as equal to them. They'll look down on me.

I can't believe this. How could my daddy, Indian himself, say this. Did his family look down on Mommy? He says no, but that was because his family was Christian, not Hindu. He tells me my mother and he had their differences to overcome. Some had to do with race, yes, but not all of it. J's family are good people, but they see the world different. I won't be accepted. Different culture. He says he's not against J. But I won't be happy. I have a different background. Different education… He reminds me J barely finish school. Look at the job he has. He's working as a security officer, doing shift work. I'm going on to University. We're from two different worlds. A marriage between us won't work out.

When I get back to my mother's house that Monday she announces a trip. To relax and take my mind off school, she's sending me to New York. It's a conspiracy, eh. Three weeks, at her sister's home. An aunt I barely know, but who's willing to host me and show me the sights. By the time I return, I'd have university registration and orientation to keep me occupied.

That don't stop me from thinking of J. Or wanting to taste and touch him. It built up like a fever. So, I look up the name of the company he's working for and call it. I ask for him. Say I'm his cousin and have an urgent family message. The switchboard girl don't believe the cousin story, but she puts me on hold to get him anyway.

He sound hesitant, guarded – because people listening. I tell him I want to see him and we agree to meet at the mall, Pizza Hut, probably. But I never get to Pizza Hut that day. I don't know if Mummy smell a rat. I tell her I going to the mall with friends to lime and have pizza. She agree, then change her mind, not giving no reason. I want to rail, but know it go make no difference. Her roof, her rules. She even put a lock on the phone, muttering about how the housekeeper tiefing phone calls. But she must have figured it out. Blasted redial!

A week later, I'm at university. Classes. New friends.

It was almost the middle of that semester when he finally find me. On his day off he take the chance and come up to the campus and walk around the food court area. I'm with a group of friends heading back to my dorm room to get some rest when I see him. He's looking sheepish. Uncomfortable. My friends were curious. I introduce him.

Polite people would have said hello and left us alone. But my friend Ian was always stupid.

He asks what the J stand for, and J very patiently tells him who Janak is in the Ram Leela. This is news to Ian, not that he's really interested. Curry was about as far as it went with him.

I'm on edge. I don't want J to think I hang out with someone as ignorant as Ian. It wasn't the first time that I realise that what in Central seems normal to me, is foreign to other students. J looks uncomfortable and embarrassed. I lead him away to a quiet corner of the food court to sit and chat. It don't go well. I sound like I'm complaining that he's come without warning; he sounds like he's whining, going on about how only bright and rich people at university. What big difference was there between our families? His parents were farmers. My father was a tradesman and my mother a mid-level public servant. It was all going wrong. I invite him to my room.

The door's hardly closed when our hands are all over each other. Youthful lust. My shirt's off, then my bra, and I'm on my bunk bed, with him on top of me fumbling with his jeans – and with mine. Then he's in his underwear. I'm completely naked. I look at him in his jockies. He looks nervous and uncertain. I help him out his shorts. He stands looking at me. You know, he actually ask me if it was too small. I didn't know what he was talking about until he gestures. I laugh and say I'm sure it isn't, but how would I know. It's obvious he thought I had boyfriends among the group, then he says that he's never been with a creole girl before. Didn't know what to expect, didn't know what I might be expecting.

Whatever we expecting never happen. Friends burst in through the unlocked door to remind me of a group project meeting. Catch us stark naked. Embarrassed and frustrated. He left. The next time I see him was months later. He's cold, dismissive. Tells me about a girlfriend he has. A girlfriend he eventually marries and has children with – as both my mother and father were happy to inform me.

So meeting fourteen years later at that fete was a bit surreal. He says he wasn't sure it was me at first. He'd been watching me casually when he recognise my features. He wasn't sure if he should approach. Suppose I didn't want to talk to him?

What was there to be angry about after all this time? So what if things hadn't worked out?

He was eager to impress me. At his friends' cooler he kept offering me drinks. Cognac? Vodka? Whisky? I decline the offers.

He looks slick. Modern. Like a magazine page. His hair styled shiny and spiky. Sunglasses even though it was 2 am. The glare from the stage, he said.

I nod. Amused.

He ask me where I working now? Say he have his own company. When I tell him I was at one of the Ministries, he turns snotty. A ministry? After all that University and studies, I was working with the government? He was sure I would have ended up in a big shot post somewhere.

He tells me how he worked security for a few years. Him and a few partners. Then it was event management. Tents, chairs, sound systems – the whole works. It was making money.

He wanted to drop me home. I tell him I'd come with friends and it'd look bad if I abandoned them. He tells me he's moved to Charlieville. Says his family did want to control him too much, which was what cause his marriage to mash up. I pretend surprise, real coy, that he'd married and he tells me the usual stuff about things going sour. He and her family don't get along. She's real controlling. They didn't click. Not like how he and me does click. Apparently, she don't even like dancing, and look how easy I lean back and dance with him.

It had felt good. He had felt good.

I take his number, and we exchange messages back and forth for a day. Until he gets fed up and shows up at my job to take me to lunch. Then to bed. It was probably the laziest afternoon, I'd had in ages. We talk and talk and talk. He admits to me that my being mixed both attracted and frightened him. His family and friends had warned him about dougla women. Hard to please. Sexually insatiable. I tell him that's a stupid stereotype. Being dougla has no bearing on sexual desire. Women want what they want when they want.

And he's okay in bed, no complaints there, but the damn man can't stop asking questions about my sex life: Eheh? How often you does want it? (As often as I can manage.) And who providing that, then? Who you having sex with? When I tell him I don't have any regular relationship, he play fast and ask if I just sleeping with any and everybody. Men and their questions too damned tedious. Even when they don't own you, they trying to own you.

I point out that we'd just had sex. Were we in a relationship? Did sleeping with him mean I had loose morals?

He drop the issue and left. I half expect to not hear from him again. But he calls to say he's home safe. Then he calls the next day to take me out again. It was a week of feting and getting home in the wee hours to make love and then head off to work. He's jumping with me for Carnival, he insists. Tells me he's just freeing himself up, he's doing what he wants now, not like when he was a child.

I joke that perhaps he's converting, but he doesn't really get it. Asks me if I want him to convert, even asks if I find him moving like a Creole. I tell him no, just moving different."

"So what happen next?"

Nicole interrupts my reverie. Lost in my thoughts.

"Well, we play mas together. Or, I did, and he jump with me. I play with Fantasy that year. I can't remember the section. It was turquoise and copper, two piece. Very revealing. One of those wire bras for the top – the bottoms covering only what was absolutely necessary. We almost miss meeting the band, because when I put it on and step out of the bathroom we end back up in bed. He even suggest we stay home instead of going out. But, I wanted to play. Whole season I waiting to play, you know?

I think the dancing with Kwesi kinda set him off. Or maybe the dancing, period. I in a band. Men will come and wine on you. They're all friends. Fellas I know, or work with or lime with. I explain it. I even try to duck some of them a little. Tell them I'm there with somebody. But is Carnival. Rum in people head. We on the road.

He try to play it off like he understand. But as the day wear on he get more and more sour. It get so bad, it spoil my

118

day. By the time I'd crossed the Savannah stage, I'm ready to go home. No last lap for me. That cheer him up because it mean he could have me to himself.

Back at my apartment he's eager to help me strip out of the costume and shower with me. After the way he behave on the road I'm not so eager. But when his hands and mouth start exploring my body, that change. We abandon the shower for bed. Then he's on top of me. Then he's talking. People shouldn't talk during sex, you know. It muddies things up. Or maybe I should say J shouldn't talk during sex. After almost fourteen years of not seeing each other, a week of bliss and a day of battling his insecurities, J's only words were: I bet them Creole and them you was with doesn't do it like this. Kwesi, who'd never been in my bed, was the only thing on J's mind. I don't know what he thinks I'd been up to in that fourteen years away from each other, but it hit me that in that week we had together he's always in a competition with somebody. Not me. To prove that he's good enough. I'm not sure why. I'm not sure what make him feel he's in a competition. I just know it isn't for me. Too much baggage.

I wish I could say that I stop him then and there. But I let him finish. Then I let him shower. Then I showed him to the door. Then I shower. Then I block his number."

THE RIGHT WORD

Mr. Grant had an affair. That's how the story starts. Now some of you will focus on the word "affair". Some of you will focus on the verb "had". A quantitative analyst might even say, "'*An* affair', so it was only one? That's good, it means he's not a serial cheater." But I want you to focus on "Mr. Grant". Why? Because if you'd met the man casually, at a soirée or something, or in a store while you were browsing for books, then you might think it extraordinary that someone like him should have an affair. To look at him, you wouldn't think sex was on his mind. He looks much more like someone who spends his afternoons curled in a comfortable chair, refreshing drink at hand, engrossed in a book than someone who fancies being comforted by an engrossing body in a refreshing way.

The other thing you need to know is that Mr. Grant is a wordsmith. He enjoys a balanced sentence with just the right amount of nuance. The perfect word in the perfect place always thrills him. It's the only way to end any conversation. He lives for picong and banter. Or at least he used to. Until last year. But we are getting ahead of ourselves. You need some context. That's another thing Mr. Grant likes. Don't just give him information, contextualize it. He needs to know the background to everything. It adds depth, he says. Keeps him in the loop. Having to rely on his imagination to fill in the blanks can be a dangerous thing, because he is blessed with a very fertile imagination. He can create scenarios that wouldn't come easily to *your* mind.

So picture a man in his early fifties. He has always led an active life, so his body is in good condition. He is trim. Lean even; he could still fit into his wedding suit. When his hair began thinning, he shaved it off and now sports a shiny bald pate, which rather becomes his bone structure.

He is neat, but not trendy. He's too preoccupied with other things to be trendy. He is strong on schedules. They are very important in keeping him in check and on track. He likes to have things neat and ordered. It makes life simple, easy to manage, when everything has its place. He has his day segmented. He knows precisely what time he's going to put the kettle on in the morning, and how many minutes later he's going to start breakfast for his family. His management of time is so impeccable he usually knows first thing in the morning what time he'll be home at night – barring any late changes on the back page's lead story, of course. As soon as he gets to work he calls his wife to let her know he's there. Mrs. Grant always knows if there's been a bad traffic jam on the highway from the timing of his call. Mr. Grant is a journalist. An assistant editor actually. In the chaos of the newsroom he is normally the area of calm. Pencils laid out neatly at the side of his computer, sharpened and ready to point out just where and how the story could be crisper, edgier, more exciting.

Melissa became Mr. Grant's pencil.

She worked the late shift as a sub-editor. He, most nights, was the last of the editors to leave. They had struck up a friendship through a shared joy in words. Not the ones tossed together on the pages in front of her, but the ones she tossed to him over their office partitions.

The newsroom was abuzz.

The toilet stalls and face basins heard everything.

"She young. Is always the young, eager ones they does go after. Look at the kind of pants and skirt she does wear to work. Is only a matter of time before she get what she looking for."

"But Mr. Grant different. He not so. He is a family man. He smart enough not to let a young girl like that distract him. I can't see him allowing she to fool up his head."

"At the end of the day, Grant is a man. You watch how she does walk around the newsroom. Hip and them swinging from side to side. Is not enough that she have the junior reporters and them running she down, she have to pick up with the editors too! What she leaving for we?"

"Oh gosh. But a married editor!"

"Melissa, you've cut this story." He was upset. If he had to re-edit the page it might throw him off his schedule. He wanted to be home by nine.

Her response was breezy, light. "I know."

"Why? The reporter is going to be pissed."

"I'm a sub, Mr. Grant. My job is to cut stories. You can consider my desk an abattoir of sorts. Good stories get trimmed, bad stories are slaughtered."

She delivered her lines over the office partition. Arms akimbo. After the parting shot there had been a half smile. The other subs had cheered. They were always fed up of the abuse dished out to them by disgruntled reporters and the pressure put on them by editors who delivered 40 centimetres when there was only room for 12 and expected the entire story, a picture, a headline and the four-column by 33 centimetre ad to fit the page. It was all numbers to the subs and words to the reporters and editors. The twain never met until Melissa. She knew words, liked them, played with them. Knew how to manipulate space to suit her needs.

He gave the page back to her. "Resurrect this story."

It was her habit to swear in French, to spare the ears of the less knowledgeable. She battled with the page for a few minutes, then gave in.

"Oh sacréfuckingbleu!" Despite the distance between their cubicles he heard her.

"A bilingual curse. I'm really sorry for that story." He chuckled quietly to himself, thinking about the use of the word sacred and fucking in the same sentence and loving the incongruity and oxymoronic nature of the obscenity. Especially if you consider that fucking can be quite sacred.

Her response was swift and took his breath away.

"No, Mr. Grant. It's just interfuckingtemesis."

At precisely that moment he fell dangerously in lust and knew he needed some context.

At 9 pm she brought him the back page, yawned, stretched, straightened and announced that she was going to get a cup of coffee. He offered to buy. She shifted her weight to one leg, causing one hip to thrust forward while she considered his offer. He had to swivel his chair away and shuffle papers pretending to consider the backpage. The intensity of his reaction was the first sign. He saw no flaws.

They bought the coffee and a cup of tea for him in silence, and drank it on the walk back to the office. After he sent the last page down to the production department he offered her a lift home. They lived in the same direction. The drive in the dimly lit car gave him the opportunity to study her features unnoticed as they chatted.

When Justine met him at the door that night he muttered about how some idiot had gotten a flat in the middle of the highway and caused a pile up like you wouldn't believe. Later that night, he found his mind drifting to Melissa. He thought of her pelvic bone in her black jeans and of the fact that guilt had made him lie to his wife when he didn't need to. The page was late through no fault of his. Why, then, did he invent that traffic jam? His wife flung her arm over him and Melissa's hip skittered guiltily out of his mind. He would stop this foolishness now.

The 9 pm coffee and the drive home became a habit. The conversations became an addiction. They would yell over the partitions in the newsroom to each other in French, Spanish, mangled Portuguese, archaic Latin and English when the other languages failed them. He discovered that they had similar tastes in films but she hadn't seen as many foreign films. He borrowed DVDs from his film club for her. They talked about the films when they went out for coffee and tea and on the drives home. Now, when he arrived at her apartment, instead of turning the car around and driving off he would park and they would talk for another twenty minutes or more. He would wait to watch her climb the stairs to her apartment. When they went for coffee he would insist they take the stairs instead of the elevator. It was good exercise.

Traffic excuses became a regular part of his life. The back pages of the paper also started going down to the pre-press department later and later. He would call to let Justine know that some damned reporter had filed the story late, or photography was still cleaning up the images or pre-press was playing the fool again. It looked like he might be late so leave the garage light on, don't bother to wait up.

He would tell his best friends that he had no intentions, good or bad. Over their beers or on the other end of the telephone they would quirk their eyebrows or the corners of their mouths. He was a grown adult. It wasn't their place to preach to him about his private life, but they saw the pattern emerging. Just give it time.

"We just have good conversations. She's really intelligent. Quick. Sharp mind."

"So you telling us all you and this girl doing is talking?"

"Yes. We've done nothing to be ashamed of. She is a co-worker. I drop her home sometimes. I drop other people home as well. No harm in that."

They were unconvinced, but silent.

He wasn't lying. But now he was careful only to offer drops to people whose homes lay before hers. It was the only way he could park and talk to her without raising eyebrows. One night she lingered, just barely, before getting out of the car. He had almost snatched her hand and pressed it between his thighs. He wanted her to know that he was still vital and capable, very capable. But by the time he had formed this thought he was watching her climb the stairs. It was a gauche thing to want to do and he was surprised, disgusted and exhilarated by his behaviour.

His wife, despite her protests, was pleasantly surprised that night.

Then two nights later, when he had decided he would make a pass at her, some idiot he was giving a lift to, Randall from pre-press, brought up the topic of his family.

"So how Justine and the children? They must be real big now. The last time I see the small one she was eleven. She must be about what, fourteen, fifteen now?"

"They fine. "He cringed. How old did she think he was? Sometimes she joked, when he missed errors, about senior moments. He was careful to tweeze the telltale greys out of his goatee, the only facial hair she could see. She had been quiet during the drive, venturing a few sentences here and there. When he dropped off the last person and was going to beckon her to the front seat he realized that she was asleep. He drove in silence to her apartment, toying with the idea of carrying her to her front step. He parked up and opened the back door for her. She climbed out sleepily and fell against him. Her body felt warm. She murmured a sorry, straightened up with some help, and then walked off. He watched her, wondering if she had noticed that he had held her hand a little longer than was necessary. He started walking back to the driver's seat and sensed rather than saw her stop.

"You not going to tell me how many children you have?"

"Three." His throat was dry.

"All of them older than eleven right?" She had the half smile on.

"All older than fifteen actually."

"I'll see you tomorrow."

But he didn't see her the next day. He didn't see her all week. He eventually asked one of the other subs, Charlene, about her. Food poisoning, she told him.

"Give her my regards when you talk to her."

"Well, actually, Mr. Grant, I'm giving her a call right now so you can tell her yourself."

Charlene was such a cheerful girl. Not terribly bright, but efficient and cheerful. He stood next to her cubicle pretending to read a page and trying to disguise his eagerness. He listened to the exchanged pleasantries, the queries about her health, the gasps of shock over how ill she'd been. At last he was handed the receiver. His voice broke on his first attempt at hello.

"So when you bringing me coffee or soup or tea?"

"Pardon." She seemed calm, matter of fact, but did sound ill and tired.

"It's been five nights since you've seen me and not a cup of coffee or a bowl of help-me-get better soup."

"You want soup?"

Charlene was watching him. He felt foolish and exhilarated.

"Is Charlene there next to you?"

"Yes."

"Okay. Well, I want soup or coffee or something. And I have your copy of *Como Agua Para Chocolate* for you to return. It's overdue a few days."

"Okay. Yes. Yes. Hope you feel better."

"What she say?" Charlene asked.

"She wants soup."

Charlene laughed. "She always hungry. Some of us passing to check her later. We will carry the soup."

He drove past her apartment three times that night. Carefully weighing in his head what he would say and do. Each time he thought how foolish he was being. He should just drive home.

"I am a married man. I am a happily married man. You are an attractive girl. But a girl nonetheless and we should keep our relationship as colleagues intact." It sounded good. Not too many words. Precise. He knocked on the door. Inside he heard a faint answer. He heard the door unlock. He watched it open. She stood in the entrance wearing a wrap and a half smile.

Later, the wrap was covering their still enjoined loins.

"I don't want to be with a married man." .

His face was pressed into her neck. He couldn't yet watch her. He couldn't yet find words to describe what had happened and he wanted to describe what had happened. He wanted to talk about it. Put it down in its exact terms. Examine it and see how it fitted into the scheme of things.

And try to answer the question that was echoing in his head: "What the hell you doing, Grant?"

"How long you married?"

"Twenty-three years."

"This is the first time you cheat on your wife?"

"No."

"I don't want to be with a married man."

"This isn't a habit of mine, Melissa."

"All I'm saying is that I don't want to be with a married man. So this is not an affair."

He pulled away from her. Her eyes were still closed. Her brows furrowed, expression serious.

"Well, what exactly is this then?"

"A mindless moment." The breeziness returned, her smile was back in place.

The moment lasted a year. The entire newsroom thought he was bewitched. Over the sputter of water in face basins and urinals you heard the talk.

"Young thing, boy, young thing!"

"Young thing, yeah, but what she see in him? She young enough to be he child. He can't handle she for too long. You see that walk she have there. That is trouble self. The man mashing up he good good living – for what? She go leave him when she get tired."

It didn't take her long to ask the inevitable. After their third encounter, with him breathing heavily beneath her, she looked him in the face and asked:

"What's the problem with your wife?"

"There's nothing wrong. Who said there's something wrong?"

"Don't bullshit me. A happily married man does not spend all of this time with a girl young enough to be his daughter."

"Are you really that young?"

"At a stretch I could be your granddaughter. So spill."

"There is nothing wrong with Justine."

"What's wrong with you then? Are you a pervert? Is it that you like really young girls, but you know it's illegal so you get someone as close to it as possible so you can fantasise? Should I put on a bib and booties next time to facilitate the ambience?"

His face registered shock. "Christ! Watch your mouth, filthy girl!"

She smiled.

"What about you? Why you with a man old enough to be your grandfather? Why aren't you with one of the young hotshot reporters?"

"Who says I'm not?"

His face fell and she hurried to dispel it. "I have an Electra Complex maybe?"

"Too pat, Melissa. Try again."

She rolled on top of him grinning mischievously and saying in a coy voice, "Perhaps I just want to be spanked. I've never been spanked you know."

In his defence he did try to be discreet and keep things hidden from his wife. His first affair had gone on for years before Justine had picked up the scent of it. When she finally accused him, he had confidently denied things because the evidence was mostly circumstantial. But then he had been able to keep things in their place and under control. This time, Justine wanted to know who was this 'Lissa he was calling in his sleep.

"Lissa? I don't know. Why?"

"Well you and she were having quite a time in your dreams last night."

It was inevitable that he would get caught. She became

a fever, a madness. He left for work at 8 am everyday. Melissa started her shift at two in the afternoon. At exactly 9:15 every morning she got a call.

"I'm in the office. Just settling down. How was your night. Slept well? I thought of you. I dreamt of you."

Her voice and body would still be sleep-warm. He would imagine that he was there with her while she yawned into his ear on the phone and told him what she had on, and then she would switch on the TV with the remote and tell him what she was watching. He would call two hours later when he came up for air from editing. By this time she would be up and about her apartment. He would ask her to touch herself. She would comply. He would sit at his desk hoping he wouldn't have to move away from it soon. Then he would call at one, just when he knew she'd be stepping into the shower. She would laugh at him and say see you soon. He'd beg her to take the phone into the shower so he could hear the water falling.

"I live in my head when I am not with you."

She would laugh and hang up.

He began going into the office for seven, working until eleven. Leaving the office for lunch and returning at one pm with Melissa in tow.

"Like they living together?"

"Nah, he still living home. But I sure the wife suspect by now."

"How you know?"

"Them reporters say she does call the office regular to speak to him and find out where he is and what time he come in and thing."

"So the showdown could be any day now?"

"I only hoping I around."

The face basins couldn't keep up with the talk. They were thankful for the moments when Melissa used the bathroom. Things became blissfully quiet.

His wife made the first move. She tried oblique first.

"You eating well these days?"

"Why do you ask that?"

"Well some days it taking you longer to digest your food than other days. Today, you were on a two-hour lunch."

"What's wrong with my having long lunch hours, Justine? You sound almost angry about that. I would have thought you'd be pleased for your husband."

But the delicate dance frustrated her. She knew the steps too well.

"Errol, look me in my face and tell me nothing is wrong. Tell me that everything is normal between us?"

"What do you think is wrong, Justine?"

"So you going to play games? You're bored again, is it? What kind is she this time? You think this one can cope with you as I do? You told her you married, I hope? You told her that this isn't the first time, I hope? God help her, Errol, because she doesn't know you the way I know you."

"Justine, I think you're letting your imagination run wild. I go from long lunch hours to having an affair?"

She eventually asked him to leave.

"It's the honourable thing to do, Errol. I don't want you here. The children and I need a place to live. You have to leave. You won't have to get out of her bed to get here before midnight. I'm sure you'll have less traffic to contend with."

★

"When are you going to get a divorce? I am not shacking up with you indefinitely, you know." It was a month now they had been living together in her apartment. She hadn't asked any questions when he turned up at her door with clothes and books in a suitcase. She made space on her shelves and set an extra plate for dinner.

If Mr. Grant was a poet he would have likened this period to spring. He made love everyday, instead of when menopausal mood swings made it possible. He discussed books, movies and music instead of domestic chores, bills and schedules. They were together constantly. At nights he kept his legs thrown possessively over her hips. He knew every twist and turn she made in bed. She would awaken every morning to find him staring at her. Sometimes he would ask her moodily, "You won't leave me, will you?"

She would smile sleepily and say, "It's my apartment. Why would I go?"

It wasn't the answer he wanted, but it sufficed.

He looked forward to every aspect of the office now. Not just the work, which could be tedious at times, but the atmosphere. The sexual energy that crackled between them, the oh-so-seemingly casual touches and glances that promised more, later. They hid nothing now. He would kiss her openly sometimes if she came up with an excellent headline or finished a sentence for him. Everyone knew. Sometimes he would absentmindedly caress her shoulders or neck while she was editing a page.

"I have thrown caution and discretion to the winds where you are concerned." Just thinking about the clichés in the sentence disturbed him. Was he now becoming a cliché. The besotted fool who is eventually left out in the cold. He thought about how easily he had left his family home. He hadn't done it the time before. Then, he had felt it was necessary to maintain a balance between his two lives. Leaving had not been an option. He thought about

Melissa leaving and became angry. He was moody for the entire drive home that night. Twice she had asked if he was okay. He had nodded and said nothing else.

When they got home she rushed out of the car and into the apartment.

"Where you going?"

She turned to him, hopping on one leg, face screwed up, "I need to pee really bad, Errol. I'm going to the toilet."

"Leave the door open, I want to see."

"What? Are you mad? Why?"

"I don't want to be separated from you ever. We must share everything. I want to see you even when you're doing things like that."

"You mad? Look, I need to pee." She closed the door.

She spent the rest of the night coaxing him into a good mood.

A few weeks later he got a call from a rival newspaper. They were offering him a job.

"If I take the job, will you come with me?"

"Where, to the other paper?"

"Yes. The salary will be higher. Or you can stop working if you want?"

"We'll still be in the same city, Errol. I like my job here. Did they say they have a position for me?"

"Well, I told them I'd move if they had a position for you as a sub-editor."

"Errol, really. You're impossible. I like it here. You should check out their offer though."

He became quiet and turned back to the page he had been editing.

He broke his silence in the car, "You don't want to leave because you like the attention in the newsroom? Isn't that it?"

"What?" She had been thinking about what to make for dinner.

"Don't think I haven't seen how the reporters look at you. How you flirt with them. That's why you don't want to move. You'll miss the attention. You can't wait for me to be out of the way so that you can carry on with them."

"Errol, I…"

"Don't deny it. There's no difference between this newsroom and any other newsroom. You want to stay because of the attention from the other men. I saw one of them chatting you up in the corner of the archives the other day. You want to fuck him, don't you?"

She was stunned.

"Why don't you save the jealous boyfriend routine for after you get a divorce? I notice I don't hear anything about that, but I get an earful about all of these nonexistent flirtations that I am having."

She gave him the cold shoulder for two days. He became melodramatic and pleaded with her to understand.

"Melissa, I'm a drowning man. Without you I have no life. I've given everything up for you. If you were to leave me I would simply sit in a corner and hope that death would come and take me."

He was allowed to touch her that night. The next day the face basins noted that everything was back to normal.

"Like it had trouble in paradise for a few days?"

"Yeah, but they back to normal now, man."

"Mark my words. Is just a matter of time."

"He would tell you that is a cliché and find a better turn of phrase."

But it took the face basins much longer to notice subtler changes. Like the fact that she didn't interact with the male

134

reporters as much anymore. The photography department and archives, once favourite haunts of hers, hardly got a visit. The head technician there had a crush on her. She wanted to avoid conflict and the constant explanations; the denials sapped her energy. The swing of her hips became less prominent and her trousers and skirts got roomier and longer. She stopped taking breaks to go and browse the city streets with the other sub-editors.

"Can't today, I have a difficult page. Maybe tomorrow."

Her phone calls became fewer. Errol got upset when she spent too much time on the phone.

"It's like you make love on that instrument, Melissa."

"I was having a conversation, Errol."

"Yes, but I was sitting right here eager to talk to you and you spent half an hour having some inane exchange about a concert, probably with one of your many admirers."

"Whatever, Errol. Whatever!"

"Nothing is ever an issue for you, is it?"

"That's not true."

"I'm voicing a concern and all you can say is 'whatever'? I wanted to talk to you urgently and you brush me off to talk about a concert!"

"I'm off the phone now, Errol. We can talk all you like."

"Well, Melissa, the moment has passed. Maybe you'll catch it the next time."

She cried in the staff bathroom and stared at herself in the vanity mirror. "What to do?" The face-basins listened to everything. But as soon as the door started opening she hastily washed her face again and left.

The call, inevitable as it was, came on a particularly bad day. There had been some suggestive comments between her and a reporter about him not having enough centimetres to fill her page that afternoon. She could tell that Mr.

Grant had overheard (she'd seen his angry glance) and was not pleased, but it didn't prepare her for the e-mail she received from him on the company's intranet.

I see that you are incapable of even mild banter now. Is your appetite for attention ever to be sated???? E.

Through blurred eyes she picked up the phone. He was looking at her from across the room. Without ever having heard the voice she knew immediately who it was.

"So, how is life?"

"Fine, I guess." She wondered what Justine could want after all this time.

"Divorce in progress yet?"

"I should ask you. It will affect you more than it will me." She hoped her voice sounded nonchalant.

"There will be no divorce, child. You didn't get him the right way. God will never reward a Jezebel."

She sighed and settled down for the sermon.

"Only a righteous woman gets a man. You don't know anything about duty, loyalty, virtue. He's done this before. But mark my words he will leave you and return to me."

It was time to end the conversation, before they got to the Book of Revelations and she became the Whore of Babylon.

"Okay. Well, since everything's inevitable, we don't need to have this conversation. You'll get your husband back, virtuous woman that you are, and I'll go to hell. Bye."

Part of her really wanted to hang up but she continued to listen to Justine's tirade.

"He'll leave. He'll tire of you. You're a child. You don't even know how to deal with his temper. Have you tasted it yet? You'll call me after you've tasted it, I'm sure. Why don't you take my num…"

She didn't need to hear anymore.

Later they were out at a restaurant having dinner.

"So, Errol, any news from the lawyers about the divorce proceedings?"

"What? No. He… ummm… he hasn't gotten back to me as yet."

"Not too pressing, is it?"

"Well… the truth is I met with him last week…"

She sighed inwardly. Here comes the inevitable plot hole.

"…and he has advised me to think very carefully about making this decision. He says lots of second marriages fail because people rush into them and so he insists I take six more months and then decide whether I really want a divorce or not."

"Oh. I see. So this is just a trial phase in our relationship then. We're not actually seriously involved. Just testing the waters, right? I see. I understand."

"Melissa, that is not what I'm saying."

"Oh yes, it is, Errol. We've been together almost a year and you're telling me you need six more months to decide whether you seriously want to divorce your wife. Or your lawyer, who seems to be a therapist as well, thinks you should take six more months to decide. And in the meantime what do I do? Twiddle my thumbs? Crochet an Afghan?"

"You could try loving me more. Loving me and only me. Stop flirting with all those other men."

Just as her pasta started losing its taste her cell phone rang. His face said, *See what I mean.* But she didn't care.

"Hello… yes, Charlene… what? Sounds fine. Can you pick me up? I'm still in the city. How about at the library steps? It's bright, busy and safe there. Ok. See you in twenty minutes."

"Where do you think you're going?" He was holding onto her handbag.

Her eyes narrowed dangerously, "Let go of my handbag, Errol. I'm going out with friends. Something I haven't done in aeons."

"No, you are not. You're coming home with me."

"I don't think so. I need about six months to decide what I want to do with my life and I think it's starting tonight. So I'm going out to meditate for a while, think deeply about my future over some drinks and a couple hours on a dance floor. See you later." She had to tug at the bag, but he let go when he realised the other patrons were staring.

Life seemed much better at three a.m. when she fumbled her way into the apartment. He was sitting at the dining table, head bowed.

"Good ni… morning." She smiled at him through the haze of coconut rum cocktails.

"I can smell you from here." His voice was low. "Where the fuck have you been?"

So this is how it's going to be, she thought. *Very well.*

"Out having a zen moment. I feel very focused and refreshed now."

"I can smell the sex on you. How many of them you fuck tonight, Melissa? One, two, all?"

"That's coconut rum you smelling, dear." She had to laugh. How dare he? He was the one talking about six months of introspection and after one night out with friends he was accusing her of cheating. Oh the irony!

As she moved to walk to the bedroom, she heard the scrape of the chair. She had hoped he would sleep on the couch. Now it looked like he wanted to bring the argument to bed. They could be up until dawn arguing this one. She would have to call in sick in the morning to get some rest.

The sudden pain was so intense she fell to the floor. Her scream was instinctive. There was a ringing in her ears. Something was stinging the back of her head. She rolled over and realized that he was hitting her. Hitting her! He was fucking hitting her! The silver serving tray from the dining table lay at her feet and he was punching her about the body.

"Errol, no!"

"You bitch! You lying conniving bitch. Coconut rum. You fuck one of them tonight. I could smell him on you. You lying to me. After all I do. I leave my family and this is what I get."

She was screaming and begging now. "Errol, no!" *My God the neighbours might hear*, she thought and actually considered lowering her voice while continuing to struggle with him. She tried crawling away from him but he sat on her and kept punching away.

She heard the words echoing in her head amid the pain. *"You don't even know how to deal with his temper. Have you tasted it yet? You'll call me after you've tasted it I'm sure."*

Then it stopped and he was lying on top of her, fumbling with her pants. It took seconds for her to register what was happening.

"Oh my God, no, Errol!"

"I have to. I have to. I have to erase all the others from your mind." He sounded like he was weeping. She lay still. It was over fast. He lay on top of her (*Was he sobbing?*) until he fell asleep. She rolled him off and went to the bathroom. Sometime later she took a knife and the silver tray with her into the bedroom and locked the door, leaving him sleeping in the corridor.

At seven she came out of the bedroom. Showered, dressed and armed. He was sitting at the table again. When he looked up he rushed to her.

"Oh my God, your face!"

She stared at him coldly. "I know. It's ridiculous the kind of garish make-up girls my age wear."

"Melissa, I'm sorry. I don't know what came over me. I was a man possessed. I promise it won't happen again."

She walked to the phone, picked up the receiver and dialled a number.

"Is that the charge room?" She put a panicked edge into her voice. He rushed at her to take away the receiver. She brandished the knife she had hidden in the waistband of her jeans and he stepped back. She spoke into the receiver in the same panicked voice. "There's an intruder in my house. I'm under the bed and there's an intruder in my house." She gave the officer on the line some more details in the same panicked voice and then hung up.

"Melissa. My God. What are you doing?"

Her tone was measured. "You are going to get out, Errol. Get out before they get here and arrest you. Because when they see my face they won't ask too many questions. Leave and stay away from me. Go back to Justine or whoever can cope with this, because I certainly can't."

"My God, Melissa. You're my life. I'm sorry. I'll make it up to you. It won't happen again. If I felt you loved me. Truly loved me. Just me. Not all the others. This would never happen. We can do couple's counselling. Yes. Let's do that. It will do you a world of good. I did it before with Justine."

She turned back to the bedroom and he followed her down the corridor. She broke into a run and managed to shut the door before he could lever it open with his weight. He called to her to open it. He didn't want trouble. Just to talk things through. She was silent. He was running out of time. The police would be there soon.

"Melissa, for God's sake. We can work this out. Just come out and talk to me. We can get past this."

He heard her laughter through the door. It was light, breezy, like their early days at the office. His heart lightened for a moment until her answer penetrated the door.

"Frankly, Errol, the moment has passed."

ACTION REACTION

It's my second day here. The policewoman and the social worker brought me. No family members. No loving, teary send off. Nobody looking as if they're sorry that I have to be here. Just two people doing their jobs and making sure all the paperwork is done.

After they left, I put up resistance to everything – which in my view is quite normal and should be acceptable. If you were in a place that you didn't want to be in, wouldn't you say you don't want to be there and insist they send you home? If you got upset enough, wouldn't you raise your voice? Maybe even bang the desk in front of you to emphasise how upset you are? But rather than seeing the logic of my behaviour, they give me injections. I really hate needles. They're so invasive. The stealthy B2 Bombers of the medical world. They go in, destroy and withdraw without leaving a trace of ever having been there. So I slept for all of the rest of my first day. This morning, even though the sedatives had worn off, I pretended to be asleep when the nurse came. She whispered to herself that I was knocked out. She saw what she wanted to see. But I'm up now and know that soon the doctor will make his way down to me. I know his steps. It's not the first time that I've been here. I know their schedule.

The walls here aren't as thin as the ones in my apartment, though I'm not sure it's still my apartment anymore.

They came and took me away from it and if I'm not there to pay the rent, I suppose it will become someone else's. But it was my apartment up until two days ago. I signed the lease and paid everything. I furnished it.

I can hear things going on in the other rooms. They forced the woman in the room to the left of mine to take her medication and to have a bath. She didn't want one. The water's too cold, she said. You have to, the nurse said. And they went back and forth until you heard the sound of metal hitting the floor and then the sound of skin slapping skin and then there were more footsteps in the corridor and more voices and the woman got her bath and was put to sleep.

I heard the doctor's voice in the room to the right of me. A low, infrequent sound. He was asking questions, but getting no response. Then I listened to the nurse outside my door saying that I was still heavily sedated and the doctor replying that he will see me on his evening round.

None of the trolleys here work properly. They have bad wheels. They're missing their rubber coating, so their metal rims scrape against the floor and screech. I hate screeching sounds. I feel like peeling off my skin when I hear screeching. I lie on my bed listening to them and I feel certain I can identify which trolley is which from its sound. One of them has all the rubber on three of its wheels, but one wheel must be damaged so there is a clanging sound it makes on every rotation. They remind me of the trolleys at the supermarket. The customers get angry with the bad wheels and then jerk them harder, as if jerking a bad trolley will make it better. It never made sense to me. They jerk and jerk the damn things as if the only way to fix a trolley is to jerk it.

I'm trying to prepare myself for later. I know what the

doctor is going to tell me. Just thinking about it makes me hot with anger. But I have to make sure I'm not angry later. Any sign of real emotion will make things bad for me. I have to be mild. When they see you are mild, they think you are sane. Only mild people are sane. Which means that at least eighty per cent of the world must be mad, because I don't think I know too many mild people. That prayer I used to recite as a child – *Gentle Jesus Meek and mild look upon this little child*. Jesus wasn't mild. He destroyed a temple. He walked all over the Middle East telling people God was his father. If I did that would anyone call me a saviour? No, they'd say I'm insane. So if I don't shout they'll think I'm normal. My boss at the supermarket should be in one of these rooms. He shouts at everyone and everything.

"Don't put the fucking box there, put it there." He doesn't even use his hands to point, so what's the difference between "there" and "there"? None. I tell him that and he looks at me funny.

"You fucking stupid?" he'd ask. "I say put it there."

I put it somewhere other than where I had it before. Sometimes I get it right with the first try, sometimes I don't. But eventually I put it where he wants it.

I had sex with him once to keep the job. He was threatening to give it to someone else. I knew that if I lost this job and had to find another one it would kill me. I didn't need that. Who loses a job packing groceries? That's what my mother would ask if I needed to borrow money from her. And I wouldn't have an answer, because I don't know anyone who has lost a job like that. I know if I tell the doctor about the sex he'll make a note on his chart and when I talk to the therapist she will tell me that I'm making bad relationship decisions, that I'm troubled about my sexuality. Which is shit, because having sex with my boss has nothing to do with sex or relationships and everything to do with survival. I needed this job to prove that I was capable of doing normal things and he needed me to screw him in order for me to keep my job. But they will say that my perception is faulty. I keep hearing that I don't perceive things the right way.

That's the reason they gave in court when they took away my children.

"She is unfit to parent, my lord. Her perception of reality is skewed. We have a report from the court-appointed psychiatrist to substantiate our claims."

It wasn't enough that I loved the children. I had to see things exactly the way everyone else was seeing them. Or said they were seeing them – because I don't think everybody sees things the same way. Isn't that why we have that saying about not seeing things eye to eye?

I let myself feel angry now. As angry as I can be so that later I won't react to them. They are always looking for a reaction. Action-Reaction, Action-Reaction, Cheryl. It was something my father used to say to me on his infrequent visits to see us. The world is physics, Action-Reaction. To every Action there is an equal and opposite Reaction. They even have a law about it.

The thing that makes me mad the most right now is a man. Not the doctor. He'll get me angry later with his bedside manner and his questions. He asks questions but doesn't really want to hear my answers. I think he could fill out his chart without actually seeing me to submit his report to my therapist. They don't care about what I have to say. It's just paperwork. There isn't even any observation. No one has come into my room to check on me at all. This is my new place. I can sense it. The same way when I moved into my apartment I knew it was my new place.

The man who gets me angry is Jackson. He works in fresh meats and poultry. I told him we had to be quiet. He's really good at slicing things up with the meat saw. He caught me watching him one day. I was fascinated with the meat saw. He thought I was watching him. Like *him*, him. But I was watching his hands. So fast, so sure. Like they knew what they were doing without needing Jackson, really. He got to like me. Most men get to like me. Then they stop.

"You give off an air of helplessness," my therapist said. She said that when I told her that men come to me; I don't go looking for them.

"You seem like a damsel in distress to them. And you are in distress, but they can't help you and they don't know that. But *you* know that, Cheryl. So you need to stop getting involved with them. You have that power. To stop these things from happening."

She doesn't understand. *I'm* not the damsel in distress. They want the help more than I do. Like with my boss. He needed the sex, I didn't. I helped him out. But it wasn't selfless. It helped me to keep my job. But it worked out well for both of us because now he thinks he's attractive again. Or something like that. We did it in the store room. He has really bad breath and sweats a lot. Women don't seem to like him much. The whole time we did it, which wasn't that long really, because I sang only one song under my breath while we were doing it, verses, chorus, bridge, and the guitar solo. So I'd say maybe four minutes. Yeah, the whole time we were doing it, he kept saying, "Tell me I could fuck good? Tell me I could fuck good?" I was humming, so I just nodded. When we were finished, I was still humming and he was really happy with himself. He said to me, "I make you sing, girl! Imagine that. You want to learn to use the cashier's machine?" But I told him no. I don't like the sound of the bell on those machines. They piss me off. Ring ring ring all the time. I hate stores because of cash registers.

So Jackson thought I liked him that day. So he started talking to me. He'd leave his position behind the meat counter and find the aisle I was restocking and talk to me.

"We have a real connection, you know."

I didn't feel it.

He tried to find out where I was living. I told him I could talk to him at work but not home. I had to be careful about home. Home had to be a safe place.

"So a big woman like you can't take home a man? I ain't dangerous. I wouldn't bite you."

I must have blushed when he said that. He said, "How you blushing so? You getting on like you was never with a man."

He said it like he knew something. I wanted to ask him about that, but I forgot. I told him I wasn't interested. But he could still walk me to my taxi-stand after work. Sometimes he would buy me something to drink, from out of the chillers at the grocery. I liked Malta the best; it was dark and smooth and frothy and sweet. He asked me why I didn't drink alcohol.

"Not even a beer self, girl?"

Beer wasn't safe, either. I didn't tell him that. I just smiled at him. I didn't tell him because he might have spoken like he knew something again, something I didn't know.

He made a noise, even though I told him about the noise. I warned him. Made him promise. I told him that he couldn't make a sound. If he promised and meant it, then and only then would I let him come to my house.

"Somebody else living there with you?"

I nodded and told him about my children. I told him how

they had taken them away from me. I told him how I had Susan when I was just fifteen and then I had Luke five years ago. Susan picks up Luke after school and takes care of him until I get home. Susan thinks she's the adult and runs the house. Sometimes, by the time the grocery closes, it's nine o'clock. I get home at ten and Luke is sleeping and Susan looks at me like I've failed at something. The same look my mother gives me. Come to think of it, they resemble. I go to my room, which is next door to Luke's, and whenever he gets up at night he'll tap on his wall. Because the walls are thin you hear every sound. I'll tap back on mine. So he'll know that I am there, that I came home. We keep tapping until sometimes I go over to his room or he comes over to mine. It's the first apartment I've had that's so big. Three whole rooms. It's run down and cheap, but I have it all to myself and my children have their own rooms. If I have a day off, I can lie in my own room and not get in Susan's way. Susan acts as if me lying down for too long means I need help. She'd be a good nurse in a place like this. The government helps me out a little and then my grocery job, and my mother helps out too. She doesn't live very far from me. She can walk to my house, as she has on a few occasions when Susan thought something was wrong and called her over. I must have been lying down too long or something and when I got up my mother was there in my apartment.

She gets angry a lot.

"You can't do without a man? You always have some man around you. You know the state you in."

I try to tell her that they follow me. I don't ask for them. They keep coming to me. It's like they need me. I don't care when they leave. But it bothers my mother a lot when they leave.

"You pick up a next one? What happen to the last one?

You even remember his name? I can't remember his name. This new one have a name?"

I think it must be important to her that I remember their names so I try. Like this meat guy. He has a high-pitched voice and vitiligo spots. So I call him Jackson, like Michael Jackson. It's easier to remember his name that way.

It was almost ten when I left the grocery that night. When I went to the store room to get more stuff for the shelves he followed me there and touched me on my arm.

"What you doing later?"

I told him I was going home. What else was there to do after work? I was too exhausted to do anything else. Packing shelves is tiring.

"We could stop for a drink by one of the bars?"

I wondered what was wrong with the drinks from the grocery. I agreed to go, but not too long. Only one Malta.

I didn't have Malta. He gave me Guinness. He said it was like Malta, only stronger. It wasn't as sweet though, so I didn't like it. But I had two because he had two beers. When he walked me to my taxi-stand I was walking a little like those trolleys at the grocery. One of my wheels gone bad.

"I promise I won't make no noise."

He was sitting in the taxi with me saying this. I told him when we got to my apartment he had to wait outside a little bit. Wait until he could come inside. He agreed. He promised again to be quiet when I asked him.

When we got home I asked for Luke.

"He sleeping, Mommy."

Susan went to bed soon after that.

I let Jackson inside and we went to my room. I gave him the sign for quiet. Shhhhhhhhhhhhhhh. Index finger on my lips. He nodded and put his finger on his lips. I was glad he understood.

I put on the radio just in case and locked the door. He would probably last two songs. Maybe three songs.

He needed me. He told me so in the bar. Several times. I asked him why? How did he know?

"You are special. Very special."

I nodded then. I understood. He recognized.

Things went bad during the second song. He wasn't being quiet. I put my hand on his mouth and he pushed it away. I put it back and then I started to hear the tapping on the wall. But it wasn't Luke, it was him. His foot was hitting the wall and he wasn't being quiet.

"You have to be quiet. You promised to be quiet."

And he started to shout Oh God Oh God Oh God. I was hearing noises outside the door and it was too much. Something was screeching in my head. The policewoman said it was the radio. She said he had kicked it off the night stand and it lost the station and was only playing static. I don't remember that. I remember screeching. My mother was at the door. Susan, couldn't you have waited? She was asking what was going on. Susan was pointing at me and then he came out of the room fixing his clothes and I knew home wasn't safe anymore and I was still hearing the screeching and I tried to stop the screeching. Luke was crying. And my mother was asking questions.

"Who is he, Cheryl? He have a name?"

I was trying to find where the screeching was coming from. They were asking too many questions. I felt like I had to hit something.

The police woman said I hit him. She said I hit him many times, with the radio and kept telling him hush. She was wrong. I told him hush first. Then I reacted. I told her there was a law about it.

SPLIT LEVEL

It's not something you born knowing. Or maybe I should say you not born knowing it.

If you had asked me then, I would tell you that Sanjay and I were the absolute same. Except that he was a boy and I was a girl. But, when you that young, being a boy or a girl doesn't much matter. You bathe, piss, shit and change clothes in front of each other all the time without really thinking about differences. He might point at your pinky, and you will point at his coco, but that was only important for when you playing dolly house, because that's how you know who had to be mommy and who daddy.

No, you don't know.

That's why twenty years later, when you're sitting in a ring around a dinner table at a writer's retreat, listening to a brown girl go on and on about the dilemma she faces being half-and-half, you think to yourself, but that is my reality… Is it a dilemma? For real?

Because, you see, here is how it goes.

You grow up in an extended household. In fact, extended might be an understatement. Your biological mother isn't there. But you have enough aunts and uncles and older cousins, either under the same roof or within walking distance of your yard, so that not having a mother around is hardly a nuisance. Besides those aunts, there is Tanty Beti, Madam Khan, Miss Zaheeda, Aunty Dulcie and Miss Felicia

– all of whom you have to pass at least twice a day if you making message by Mr. Greenidge shop or going by Aunty Marjorie with a parcel. In truth, all of Jerningham Junction Road, at least the stretch you live on and traverse daily, parents you. You do aarti puja when you feel like it in Tanty Beti yard with Sanjay's older sisters Girlie, Girlin and Dolly. Uncle Fat Boy Sultan, who is your Uncle Lum Loy's most faithful card partner, brings sawine and penuz for you all the time. At least, you think it's all the time. It's really once a year. But you see Uncle Fat Boy every day; you have to pass his house. You see him on his way to and from Masjid all the time. Salaam, Uncle. Salaam, daughter.

When your mother does arrive for those infrequent midweek visits, it's an inconvenience for you. Your aunt, the woman you think of as mother, spends all morning nervous as hell, combing your hair, oiling your limbs, searching you for scars and marks. If she finds any, she frets even more. You hate washing and combing your hair. It's long, thick and bushy. You know because your aunt complains bitterly while combing it out and putting it into loose corkscrews.

Sanjay is standing at the tank that you just dipped water from to bathe, asking your aunt if you can come over and play. He has new ducks. Aunty shoos him away.

Her mother coming, boy, you can't see she will be busy?

It sounds ominous. You are a bit scared. Even noisy Uncle Lum Loy, who rules the house with his shouts and curses, seems a bit put out by the visit.

When she comes, you are inspected.

How she hair looking so? Why you don't plait it properly? Is only corkscrews you know to put it in?

It wash today. The corkscrews is to let it dry out properly without it getting too bushy.

Hmphhh. Is only when I coming her hair does wash?
We wash it weekly.

Who is we? I ain't want any and everybody putting their hand in my child hair you know.

And that's how it goes between the adults. You are given a present which you graciously accept. Acceptance means suffering an awkward hug and sitting quietly with the adults when what you really want to do is carry the present across the road by Sanjay so you can show him whatever is in the box – it's shoes this time – and play with his ducks.

Your mother leaves and the house exhales.

Your father, who has been out all day installing cupboards, gets home at about six pm. This is a good time because you're starving and everyone has been waiting for him to get back to have supper. The aunts want to tell him about your mother's visit. You sit on his lap and eat. Aunty has made a channa punch to go with the sada roti and fried plantains for dinner. Your roti is soaking with butter. Daddy takes a piece of your plantain. But you do not mind. You love this man who smells of sawdust all the time, and whose smile is wide and toothy just like yours. You curl up next to him every night and ask many questions – even while he is asleep, because he answers even in his sleep. It is the same bedroom you once shared with your grandfather – the grandfather who let you sip rum from his cup every day because it was good for the worms, the grandfather who made dental plates for almost all of Lendore Village, Warrenville and Cunupia, the grandfather who was back in this bedroom the evening after his funeral, talking to you like he'd never been gone. He still in that bedroom all now.

And even then you don't know.

You certainly don't know when you start primary school and Amawattie becomes your best friend for all the first year. You try hard to help her with her lessons, but she doesn't learn to read, spell or count as quickly as you do, and she learns to resent you for being quicker than she is with your tables. You can't help it. Aunty makes you sing tables all the time in the kitchen. It's a game you play while you make kurma or fried channa for the Saturday church snack. And you sit on your father's lap while he is reading. That's your first memory of reading, on his lap.

By second year, Amawattie no longer talks to you about anything. Not even *Sheriff Lobo* or *Fall Guy*. Joyce becomes your friend. You're both at the same reading lesson, and can recite up to four-times tables easily. You play hand games, recite tables, spell words, or talk about *Sheriff Lobo*. Joyce wears brown canvas Jim Boots to school. You wear white ones. You walk home together after school, swinging hands. Joyce's mother, Aunty Indira, meets her half way every day, at the point where you separate on the main road to turn into Jerningham Junction Road. Uncle Harry is usually sitting on his porch at that hour and he tells you when to cross.

One day the aunts are talking in the kitchen. Low voices. They sound concerned. Something is wrong. You walk into the kitchen trying to pretend you don't know something is up. You ask for something to eat. Aunty Marie, the young easygoing one, asks a question.

How you would feel about going to live with your mother?

Aunty Olive is my mother. I not going anywhere. Why?

Panic creeps in. Aunty Olive is crying. She has been crying for some time, but you only now realize that her eyes are red and her face is wet. Because she is crying, you cry. Who would dare make this woman cry? You cling to her. Bitter tears run down your face and you are not even certain why.

Even then, you don't know. But you are coming to a time when things make themselves clearer.

Soon, much bigger words than the Nelson West Indian Reader contains become a part of your vocabulary: separation, mortgage, reconciliation, split-level.

You leave this world of countless aunts, uncles and cousins and go to live with just your mother. Who comes from a different world. Who was separated from your father, though you can't remember them ever having been together. But they own a house together. A whole house. A big house. A mortgage has to be paid on this house. It is a split-level. They are giving marriage one more try. A reconciliation. You didn't even know you had married parents. Aunty Olive was your mother and Daddy was your daddy.

In this new house, on this new street, you don't talk to anyone. Except to say good morning or good evening to people whose names you don't yet know. There is a Pentecostal church that has service all day on a Sunday. But you see no mandirs or mosques.

The next door neighbour has three children. You can only speak to them when your father is around and in the yard.

Your mother has warned you to not play with them.

Their mother too fast. She always want to know my business. I don't want no coolie knowing my business.

They don't speak properly, she says. You don't speak properly either. She complains bitterly about your singsong voice.

Just like your father family.

There is always a new word to learn with your mother. You say cocoyea, she says flex broom. You say bilnah, she says rolling pin. You say tawah, she says platine.

What is a coolie, you ask her.

The people next door, she says. And the way she says it, you don't feel being a coolie is a good thing.

One day, you find yourself by the drain that separates your yard from the neighbour's. The children are in the yard. Your mother is inside taking a nap. You take the chance to talk. Soon you are tearing up the pages of an old copybook making paper boats and racing them in the drain. You are laughing, chatting, exchanging secrets. Before you know it, you are asking them the question that has been plaguing you. What is a coolie? The eldest child looks at you funny. And then she answers. Like us. Like your father.

You continue to play. But in your head you are confused. Your father is a coolie? But your mother says coolie as if it is a bad thing. Is Aunty Olive a coolie too? And Tanty Beti, and Uncle Fat Boy… and Sanjay?

You ask another question. Is my mother a coolie?

They laugh at you. No, she is a negro, girl. How you stupid so?

So, I am part coolie?

Yes.

Your father finds you that evening sitting in the back yard deep in thought. Your mother is none the wiser that you have played with the children next door, or that you have all this new information.

He sits next to you, taking off his work shoes, knocking off the fine sawdust.

What you do today?

You tell him the truth, because already there is a tacit understanding between you and him about HER.

I play with the children next door.

Eheh? What all yuh play?

Boat racing in the drain.

Your mother know?

No.

Ok.

Daddy?

Yes?

Am I a coolie?

Where you hear that word?

From Mommy.

His face darkens. You get uncomfortable. Because he never gets angry. But right now is the angriest he has ever looked.

Eventually he answers you. His face no longer angry.

No, dear. You are mixed.

And even then, you don't really know.

CALENDAR OF EVENTS

In Nineteen Episodes

1. Isabella

Isabella has always been an island of transhipment. People and goods. The people Columbus met here were adept at remaking temporary civilisations as they moved further north or south, as the need arose. Raleigh and his peers did much the same. Isabella became the convenient port of call between the myth of El Dorado and the hard truth of the metropolis. In fact, Isabella grew accustomed to the role of loyal side chick. Always there. Always willing. Always able. On the surface, cheerful and carefree. Hiding the insecurities and bitterness that such transient attentions nurture. Helping her metropolitan man to achieve greatness and amass wealth without ever being able to lay claim to any of it. In short, the movement of people and goods, legitimate or otherwise, is the foundation of Isabella.

2. A Prime Minister, an Announcement and a Heist

On the evening of January 24th, 2015, at 9 pm, five years after having become the first female leader of her political party, the Prime Minister of Isabella, speaking to the media on her way into the first fete of the Carnival season, announced that April 20th, not May 24th as the Venezuelan seer was predicting, would be the date of the upcoming general elections. The date, she said, had been arrived at after lengthy Cabinet discussion and deliberation. What she didn't mention was that while the Cabinet met in its normal room at the Office of the Prime Minister, she had excused herself to consult privately with her spiritual adviser on the most auspicious date.

Eight hours later, when she was tucked into bed, confident victory would be hers, a $25 million dollar heist took place. That, at least, was what the newspapers reported.

3. Ryan Indarsingh, a Panel Van and Two Dead Armed Guards

Ryan Indarsingh aged overnight. Twenty-five million dollars stolen from a truck, and two armed guards shot dead. The driver had been instructed to use a panel van to move the money instead of one of their heavy-duty armoured trucks, because Ryan didn't want to draw attention to the vehicle. It had two pick-ups to make that night. One collection was at the fishing depot in Cocorite; the other, the cash at the bank. An armoured truck at a bank wouldn't raise eyebrows, but one at a fishing depot in the middle of the night surely would.

The country was wild with curiosity over the news of the heist. The murdered men's families were wild with grief and need. They were the household breadwinners. Was the company going to compensate? It was all Facebook and Twitter seemed to talk about. The election date became important only to those facing re-election. People began posting home-made re-enactment videos online, and everyone agreed that workers inside Amalgamated Banking, whose money was being transported, must be in on the heist.

In those early days Ryan barely had a moment to think. He simply reacted. There was the police investigation, the funerals to support and the general media circus to navigate. There was also the matter of the rest of the cargo, Mr. Adam's fifteen million, to locate. He hadn't yet discussed the matter with his partner, Marvin Gonzales.

4. Candice and a little Back Story

Candice, not her real name, is a journalist. She likes seeing her name in by-lines. Likes the media passes. The complimentary meals. The private phone numbers of sources who always eventually need a solid favour done in the newspaper. The only thing she hates about her job is having to do research. But Candice had a friend, a friend called Asha. Again, not her real name, but what is real anymore? Asha was one of those bright, resourceful types that everyone should have as a friend – or occasional outside woman. Working hard, but earning little. Wanting a change. A new job, a new life. She is considering leaving her job in banking to manage a hotel. An occasional lover has made her an offer. He wants to get into the hotel business. He is sorting out the capital. He wants someone bright, who pays attention to detail, like him. She is tempted, very tempted. Until that happens she lives here plotting ways to escape into her imagined life. She helps Candice, because Asha likes research. Collecting information. Making links. Knowing things. Asha often has something interesting to email Candice. The other thing they have in common is Marvin, but only Asha knows this.

5. Ryan and Marvin: a Longish History

Ryan had always been street smart. One does not grow up in an orphanage run by Presbyterians in a country like Isabella without learning to take on Anansi forms to survive. Ryan learned to shapeshift from young. To fit in as much as possible. If we had to pin his personality down to an element of the zodiac or the Chinese horoscope, Ryan was surely a water sign. Marvin, on the contrary, was a block of wood. Solid, useful, amazing to look at when polished the right way.

Marvin and Ryan met at youth camp. Ryan had been one infringement away from being sent to juvenile prison. Marvin was both unlucky and lucky to be there. His father had left home, when Marvin was four, to live with a Jezebel Whore of Babylon, as his mother called her. This same mother had several misters herself, one of whom was a community police officer and a bully. He used his skills as a bully to beat Marvin's mother and his influence as a police officer to have Marvin shipped off to the youth camp in Persto Praesto after the second occasion on which Marvin dared to square off to him in defence of his mother. But, as we know, police officers are selected from only the best, most reasonable citizens, and little black boys between the ages of 15-24 from single-parent homes are the greatest criminal threat facing humanity. After that second fight in defence of his mother, Marvin earned the titles of "gang member", "known to the police" and "community pest". He had the brief fame of a small blurred picture of himself coming out of court in a news story titled, "Cunupia Schoolboy Terrorises Community Police"; he was referenced in a Facebook thread dedicated to bashing him along with "them youths today" and the wickedness of "little black boys"; and a sentence of two years in a camp to teach him discipline. His mother's plea, "He's a good boy", was met with derision. Everybody knows that black single-parent women spend all their time breeding children but not necessarily minding them. In truth, Marvin was lucky. A different police officer might have raided his home, planted weed and shot him in self-defence.

While masquerading as up-and-coming menaces to society, at youth camp the two learned to check for each other, to protect each other's backs to the point of insepa-rability. They learned to work with their hands: farming, some sewing, woodwork, masonry, plumbing. Marvin, who paid great attention to detail, excelled at practical tasks; Ryan became a genius at cutting corners. When the two of them were released from the camp, it was Ryan who secured work for them as skilled craftsmen with a fly-by-night construction company, and Marvin whose skill and attention to detail kept them hired. When the boss short-paid them for their labour, it was Ryan who made up for the shortfall by devising ways to steal materials and tools from the construction site and do private jobs on their weekends and evenings. It was Marvin's steadiness that ensured they saved more than they spent.

It was after a long weekend of liming and drinking, that a hungover Ryan hit upon the idea.

"We should start we own company."

"Eh? How?"

"That girl in the party this weekend. She working local government. She in the section that does handle contracts and bids for public works. She was talking about how easy it is to get a contract."

"The one you went home with?"

"Not home, we went by she car. But yes, she. We just

need somebody on the inside to hand we bids and proposals to. And we could hand it to her. She will put it on the right desks. But we need a registered company."

"But how we starting that?"

"Easy, we need two or three partners to name as directors down in the Registry… and…"

"And what?"

"We need some money."

"We have money."

"I need a partner I could trust." Ryan then hit Marvin a meaningful look. "You know anybody I could partner with?"

"You like to talk shit, eh?" was Marvin's response.

Three months later, they walked away from their day jobs with a quarter of the construction company's staff. This was November, 2010. A year later, Praesto Construction had become an umbrella organisation that comprised construction, landscaping, tent and party rentals and building maintenance. Two years later, Praesto realised that the sites they built, buildings they maintained and parties they supplied tents for needed security. So they started another company, separate from the Praesto group of companies, and with different directors.

That Christmas, of 2013, Ryan bought matching Range Rovers for himself and Marvin, with the license plate numbers 10 and 11.

"Why 10 and 11?"

"November 2010."

"Eh? I not understanding."

"The month and year both of we walk away from poverty, man. So 10 and 11. The two vehicles in both of we name. Drive whichever one available."

6. Drew, Things, a Contact List and Stacy

Drew is officially Andrew. By day he works as a courier for a car distributorship – Prestige Motors, a subsidiary of Prestige Holdings, importers of BMW, Jaguar and Range Rover. When the client drops off a car for repairs or tune-ups, it is Drew's job to sign out an appropriate company car to prevent their clients from being inconvenienced on their daily errands. Through the clients he meets and his ready access to transport, Drew has also become a purveyor of things. He can pick up and drop off at will. His iPhone's contact list is something he is proud of. It makes him a popular guy. Sometimes, when he is driving his big shot clients he tries to impress them with the people and things he knows.

Stacy is a girl on his contact list. He often drops her home in the wee hours of the morning when she has finished work at the Hyatt. The Ministry covers that tab. One night, Drew is asked to pick up Stacy and take her to a meeting.

7: Stacy, a Skill and Matters to be Recorded

Stacy is cute. Stacy's so cute that she gets free tickets to everything that opens. Especially doors. Doors to penthouse suites in hotels frequented by government ministers. Stacy spends a lot of time being cute in these penthouse suites. But, sometimes, Stacy gets bored with being cute and she does non-cute things like lime with friends from the old days on the Avenue, get stupidly drunk and forget her phone in their cars. Drew is an old friend. He returns phones, but sometimes it takes a few hours because he's curious about what can be found on them. Delays can be costly.

Before Stacy went to that meeting, she did a few things that might interest us. She lived in Tacarigua as a child. Developed a healthy appetite for sex as a teen. Got a job at the Ministry of Local Government's Works Office. Caught the Minister's eye. Had sex in her car at a fete one weekend with a childhood crush. Helped him get a start-up business off the ground. Had sex with the Minister. Often. Took pictures of it. Often. Sometimes she let the Minister and his friends snort lines off her belly, while taping it. She was also helped to set up a few companies in her name that she knows very little about beyond the money that shows up regularly in her bank account – for her trouble. The directors of the companies, our friends Ryan and Marvin, handle all practical matters. Stacy would tell you that these companies were responsible for "shipping and transporta-tion". In Isabella's street corner thesaurus, these terms had quite a different meaning.

8. Candice, Mr. Adam and an Interview

Mr. Adam agreed to give Candice the interview because it was good PR for his business community. With all the unrest in the eastern commercial district – petty traders being ousted in favour of gyro carts; a growing community of illegal immigrants from other islands sucking up menial jobs and lowering the cost of labour; and the daily murders – someone had to say something positive about business and commerce in the city.

Mr. Adam, as the eldest son in his generation, told Candice the story of the three generations of his family in the Caribbean, beginning with his grandfather's humble arrival in 1905 off a boat that needed repairs. Of his seeing

Port of Spain for the first time; of selling his wares off a bicycle, then from the back of a car, and eventually in a shop, which became a department store, which expanded into the corporation now rebranded as Prestige Holdings. It was a pull-up-by-the-bootstraps sort of story. A tale of hard work, thrift, abstinence and sacrifice.

As Candice idly made notes, she thought, without any real rancour, it was a story she had heard before, except her thrift, abstinence and sacrifice, and that of her mother and her mother's mother, hadn't managed to make *her* family one of the wealthiest in the country, in just three genera-tions. She mentally noted the businesses Mr. Adam talked about. The clothing boutiques, the chain of pharmacies and coffee shops. He didn't explain how the pharmacy and coffee shop chains generated such high profits and kept spawning new branches, despite high prices and low customer turnover. He avoided discussing the under-the-counter drug trade in the pharmacies, or the Town and Country bylaws his shops broke or bypassed because of his close relationship with the Minister of Local Gov-ernment – whose last campaign he had financed. He didn't mention his legal and above board security firms that were now in high demand all over the country – demand raised by the alarms over gangs, turf-wars, blocks, corners and murders – or the "shipping and transporta-tion" operations that lay behind them. This was meant to be a feature story celebrating the country's diversity, not an article discussing business in all its manifestations. So, he talked about growing up in a multilingual home, of being part of a migrant minority and loving Isabella just as much as everyone else who was here, and how much employment he created for black communities. Several times. And, as a closing declaration, in the light of the season that was now upon them, how much he loved calypso and supported pan.

At the end of the interview he asked casually, jocularly almost, "All yuh reporters must have all the inside information in the world, eh? What is the real story behind yesterday's heist, girl?"

"No clue, nah, Mr. Adam. Even police stumped. I not covering it; another reporter covering it. And from what I hear, no leads thus far."

"Helluva thing, eh girl. Twenty-five million disappear just so, just so? Is just twenty-five million, ent?"

"From what I've heard, yes. Why?"

"As a businessman, I have my concerns, girl. I have my concerns. It could have been my money, eh?"

9: Marvin and a Delayed Realisation

It seemed to take Marvin almost two days to realise that he was linked to the heist, before he spoke to Ryan about it. He had been busy, he told Ryan. Construction was booming; he was busy managing multiple jobs on multiple sites. Ordering materials, managing workmen and keeping up with the accounts. He and Ryan had long since divided the responsibilities in their business, with Marvin functioning as chairman of the group of companies, throwing an eye on the accounting and human resource issues every so often, and overseeing the construction side of things. Ryan, always a hands-on quick thinker, was CEO and handled the day-to-day running of the security business.

That Tuesday, when they could finally talk privately, Ryan didn't disguise the fact that matters were grim.

"It worse than just the guards who get shoot, Marvin."

"You mean the money? Banks insured that. That will get covered."

"Is not just the money."

Marvin looked steadily at Ryan. "What you mean?"

Ryan told him.

Money. Cocaine. And three women.

9. Candice, Marvin and Asha

Candice had a bath and was engaged in mild sexting with Marvin for the better part of an hour before slipping in the question about the photograph. The pic wasn't his, he said. He'd been sent it by a "friend". She closed off the chat when Asha's messages began coming in.

AshaB: Your girl has an interesting background.

CanDid: You mean because she dates ministers?

AshaB: That's the dull part. Nothing hard about dating a minister. That's the only way those men can get sex! Nobody would sleep with them otherwise...

CanDid: Lol...

AshaB: Your girl is your average government clerk, clocking an 8 to 4, making enough to pay a rent but not enough to qualify for a mortgage... but she's also, if my eyes are to be believed, a wealthy business woman.

CanDid: Huh?

AshaB: Yep. According to the Companies Registry, she owns a few businesses. In the areas of cargo and transportation mostly.

CanDid: What?

AshaB: Yep. And that's only the start. Their boards of

directors have names that, strangely enough, match the last names of the Minister of Local Government.

CanDid: You lie!

AshaB: If I'm lying, blame the Companies Registry. But, there's more. I put the addresses for the company in Google Maps… They're both private condominiums in gated communities. Unless Google Earth is lying, nothing remotely resembling construction or cargo consolidation is happening at those addresses. Just pools, playgrounds and apartments.

CanDid: So fake companies?

AshaB: Fake might be inaccurate. Money passing through the companies according to the declarations of companies sub-menu on the Inland Revenue website. They've declared their profits and paid their taxes. So money is passing through them. If they're legitimate, then those addresses and phone numbers are wrong.

CanDid: Hmmmmm. Anything else?

AshaB: Yes. Her name is also down as owner of two state-built homes.

CanDid: Oh my God! She's got two state houses?

AshaB: And is probably acting as the front to a government minister. I'd suggest checking to see if the Ministry uses that transportation and cargo consolidation firm. And how often. The office address is Cocorite. You could also check out her profile on Facebook. See who she takes selfies with. Try and establish if those company directors are indeed related to the Minister. Didn't your paper do a profile on him when he was elected? There must be bio-data floating around. It's 2 am, I've got to sleep.

CanDid: Ok. Thanks. Will tell you what I dig up tomorrow.

AshaB: You mean today. Is gone after 2 am. 'Night.
CanDid: Lol. G'night.

11: Asha and Candice Again

By 10 am the following morning, Asha had inboxed more information to Candice that established links between the grinning Minister, Stacy, the condominiums and their use as a private member's club in the midst of a residential community. The documents included photographs of people entering the premises, cadastrals of the condominium development, registration documents for a private member's club in the Companies Registry and one page from a dated police report of complaints from residents about the activities at the condominiums.

Asha: I think what I've found for you is going to blow the heist story out of the water. You have a government minister snorting lines off his employee and a private members' club all linked together.
Candice: What? Where?
Asha: Open the documents I just sent you. You'll want to print them discreetly.
Candice: Hold on, they downloading. Not opened yet… Okay, they opening up… Dear God…. where did you get these?
Asha: Can't say. Just remember my name is still, "a well-placed, anonymous source".
Candice: I not going to question a gift horse. And you right. This makes the heist story fade into distant memory.

At this point, the alert reader should perhaps be asking who might have an interest in the heist story disappearing.

12. A Stomach and a Blurred Face

On Saturday January 31st, the headlines blared: "Blurred Lines", and featured a photograph of a line of cocaine on what looked like someone's stomach and a blurred, grinning face. The story alleged that someone resembling "a high-ranking government official" had been "caught in a digital image", whose source was anonymous, "possibly inhaling a white powdery substance in the presence of a female companion". The one thing the newspaper was certain about was that the stomach featured in the picture belonged to a female companion. No one questioned the gender of the stomach.

Radio deejays played the Robin Thicke song that shared a title with the headline every hour on the hour and conducted random polls asking the public who they thought the high ranking official could be.

On social media, bloggers and activists immediately called for the Prime Minister's head and asked that she and her Cabinet step down.

Supporters of the government countered that the image was Photoshopped, that it was two different blurred pictures brought together and how could we be sure that the powdered substance was illegal. The makers of memes fired up their generators and nearly broke the internet that night with images of every government minister snorting lines of cocaine off the stomach of the female companion.

13: The Minister, Shaved Genitals and a Hotel

On Sunday February 1st, the Minister's face became much clearer on the front page of the newspaper; and on pages 3 and 5 the lines of cocaine and the female companion's shaved genitals, thought to be a stomach the day before, were now in sharp focus. There were accompanying photos of the Hyatt Waterfront hotel rooms in broad daylight – to show that the fixtures and fittings in their penthouse suite rooms were those featured in the picture with the smiling minister.

Bloggers renewed their calls for the Prime Minister and her corrupt cabinet to step down. This straw would surely break the camel's back.

The nation must be ready to march, statuses shouted.

The Opposition joined the chorus. Weighty comments were made. Tweets and Facebook statuses were posted, shared, retweeted, edited and shared again.

Government supporters went into a huddle. They returned late Sunday afternoon with an image they had Photoshopped of the Opposition Leader shooting up heroin in a dingy room. Bloggers called it their Photoshop argument.

Radio deejays asked callers to guess how many days before the minister would be fired. Text messages to the Minister's phone went unanswered. John Public wondered whose pussy it was in the picture and who had done the expert wax job. Lord Kitchener's "My Pussin" enjoyed a brief revival, as did lame jokes about cats.

The Office of the Prime Minister remained silent.

14: Stacy, the Minister, Candice and a Sudden Departure

"Private Members" was Monday's headline. It featured another three-page investigation complete with pictures making the links between the Minister, Stacy and their shared business interests. The Praesto Group was not mentioned. All by-lined to Candice Donaldson.

The heist update had been relegated to a few paragraphs on page 17, close to the editorial and opinion columns.

Within an hour the meme generators had been fired up and the citizens of Isabella weighed in on the matter. The Minister couldn't be found for comment. Stacy's office and townhouses were staked out. Civil society groups called for the Minister's resignation on radio and television talkshows.

At this point, the Prime Minister flew to Costa Rica to deliver a speech at an environmental summit. Her decision to go had not, previously, been announced. Editorials noted, tongue-in-cheek, that in flying off to save the earth, the PM was in fact flying off to save her skin.

15: The PM and a Conference

Talk Radio found new ways to ask the same question each morning: "Would the Prime Minister fire the Minister?" Media houses reported that the PM was refusing to respond to emails, texts and calls on her official accounts.

The PM finally responded: *On my way to Conference in Costa Rica. See Press Release. Haven't seen media reports. Will catch up on flight.*

The conference lasted three days, but the Prime Minister extended her trip into a state visit and stayed for five extra days.

New memes, tweets and Facebook updates were posted. Radio and television shows devised poll questions concerning the Prime Minister's overseas trip, pending return and ability to make decisions and account to the public.

In a press release on her official Facebook page, the PM

assured the nation that she was on an important and necessary state trip to forge ties with a trading partner. Ties that could lead to jobs in the environmental sector. However, the press release continued, the Prime Minister would, upon landing, address matters of serious concern to the nation.

16: The Minister in Question

When reached for comment, the Minister asked the reporter to prove that it was his face in the picture. He also said that he would be among the dignitaries greeting the Prime Minister upon her return from Costa Rica.

17. The Prime Minister and the Nation

The Prime Minister's private jet arrived at 7:30 pm. News stations had been on stand-by for her address to the nation since 7 pm. However, the tassa and African drum band that had been contracted to greet the Prime Minister on her return had a flat tyre on the road, which delayed them by fifteen minutes. Then there was the clearing of security and the time needed to set up the ensemble on the tarmac in proper health and safety garb.

At 8:10 pm, the Prime Minister finally disembarked from the plane, accompanied by her spiritual adviser and a crescendo of drums. Her Minister of Communication gave welcoming remarks and stated that the Prime Minister was exhausted from her gruelling journey and would not be taking questions. He also distributed press kits announcing the PM's social agenda for the upcoming week.

The meme generators began warming up.

When the Prime Minister finally came to the podium, she announced a change in proceedings, and invited her Minister of Legal Affairs to say a few words – because someone was still fetching her glasses. The Minister of Legal Affairs spoke for approximately six minutes outlining the latest legislative bills tabled for Parliament. None dealt with misbehaviour in public office or a drugs policy for elected officials. By the end of his speech, three memes were already circulating on Facebook. One depicted the Prime Minister wining to tassa at a chutney fete with the caption, "Ah Reach!"; another showed an old woman with false teeth perched atop her head with the caption, "I need my glasses to find my teeth"; the third meme poked fun at the Minister of Legal Affairs and his empty list of legislation.

When she finally spoke, the PM announced that her speech was entitled "A Greater Accountability". For fifteen minutes she berated the local media for putting scandal before well-researched journalism. She named news articles, editors and reporters in her speech. Urged them to make "well-researched, investigative journalism" their focus and to stop "dogging and demonising" her government. In just one sentence she mentioned briefly that she had accepted the resignation of her Minister of Works and that she would now take over this portfolio until such time as she saw fit. Then she continued to discuss the behaviour of reporters and those employees in Ministries who were seeking to undermine her government by becoming "intimately involved" with the media, while they were meant to be performing their professional duties.

She challenged the editors to publish only "newsworthy and noteworthy" stories. Stories that would uplift the nation. She ended her speech by wishing the nation a safe Carnival season.

18. The Newspapers and a Social Calendar

"Prime Minister to Fete All Week" was the next day's lead story. The entire social calendar from the Office of the Prime Minister was printed complete with state letterhead. The page three story indicated that the Prime Minister would be attending three parties, and that the information in the story had been researched, crosschecked and verified by two reliable sources: the Prime Minister's press secretary and her Minister of Communications.

Pages five and seven carried stories about the minister being fired for drug use and misbehaviour in public office.

Page nine had a brief article about the leads having gone cold on the $25 million dollar heist.

Page eleven carried two paragraphs about unidentifiable human remains discovered in the burnt-out shell of a Range Rover.

19: The Election

At 12:15 pm the Prime Minister released the announcement that Parliament was dissolved. Elections were now due in five weeks.

Someone naive might conclude that had Candice Donaldson been an investigative journalist and not just a reporter, she would have gathered her own information on Praesto Construction and its owners, Ryan Indarsingh and Marvin Gonzales. She might even have stumbled upon a paper trail that showed Marvin had recently invested in a newly-formed chain of Caribbean hotels that catered to elite, exclusive tastes. These hotels prided themselves on their discretion and ability to provide whatever their clients needed to relax. She might have questioned, too, the coincidence of Asha's migration to a new job further up the string of islands to manage a chain of hotels; or the rapid cooling off between her and Marvin. But he had no more juicy information for her anyway.

She might have done these things, but we know why she didn't, and why the story of a $25 million dollar heist (we talking US here), disappeared from the news. You might be feeling just a tiny bit sorry for the minister who was sacrificed for enjoying a little middle-aged vanity. Don't. There were company directorships for him. Who you can be sorry for is a dead girl with a misplaced phone who didn't really understand what she was getting into; a company driver with bigshot ambitions, a big mouth and little sense; two armed guards and us Isabellans, who have only an election to look forward to.

ABOUT THE AUTHOR

Rhoda Bharath is a Caribbean author, who teaches and blogs about politics and culture in the hours between night and day. Having parents from both islands that make up the union that is Trinidad and Tobago can be culturally complex enough. Add multiple ethnicities to the mix and you get Rhoda Bharath. In 2002 she was a participant in the Cropper Foundation's Caribbean Residential Writer's Workshop. On the heels of that experience she pursued her MFA in Creative Writing at the UWI, St Augustine Campus and completed it in 2007. Thereafter, she went on to be actively involved in the writing programmes at the University of the West Indies, COSTAATT and on the organising committees for the Cropper Foundation and the Bocas Literary Festival in Trinidad and Tobago. She was shortlisted for the Hollick-Arvon Prize in 2014 for Creative Non-Fiction Writing. She teaches English Language, Literature and Creative Writing for a living; and blogs to keep sane. When she isn't writing or teaching she is actively involved in managing mischief.

Barbara Jenkins
Sic Transit Wagon and other stories
ISBN: 9781845232146; pp. 180; pub. July 2013; price: £8.99

"Barbara Jenkins writes with wit, wisdom and a glorious sense of place. In stories that chart a woman's life, and that of her island home, this triumphant debut affirms a lifetime of perceptive observation of Caribbean life and society."
— Ellah Allfrey, Deputy Editor of *Granta Magazine*

The stories deal with the vulnerabilities and shames of a childhood of poverty, glimpses of the secret lives of adults, betrayals in love, the temptations of possessiveness, conflicts between the desire for belonging and independence, and the devastation of loss through illness, dementia and death. What brings each of these situations to fresh and vivid life is the quality of the writing: the shape of the stories, the unerring capturing of the rhythms of the voice and a way of seeing – that includes a saving sense of humour and the absurd – that delights in the characters that people these stories.

Elizabeth Walcott-Hackshaw
Mrs. B
ISBN: 9781845232313; pp. 236; pub. 2014; price: £9.99

"...richly entertaining... offers a vigorous, at times sizzling, prose that is grounded in local rhythms and allusions to the culture that is at once both the object of her love and also her main target."
— Arnold Rampersad, *Trinidad Guardian*

Ruthie's academic success has been Mrs. B's pride and joy, but as the novel begins, she and her husband Charles are on their way to the airport to collect their daughter who has had a nervous breakdown after an affair with a married professor.

Loosely inspired by Flaubert's *Madame Bovary*, Mrs. B focuses on the life of an upper middle-class family in contemporary Trinidad, who have, in response to the island's crime and violence, retreated to a gated community. Mrs. B is fast approaching fifty and Ruthie's return and the state of her marriage provoke her to some unaccustomed self-reflection. Like Flaubert's heroine Mrs. B's desires are often tied to the expectations of her social circle.

Sharon Millar
The Whale House and other stories
ISBN: 9781845232498; pp. 168; pub. April 2015; price: £8.99

A pathologist is asked to lie about a boy killed on a government minister's orders; a sister tries to make peace with the parents of the white American girl her brother has murdered; a gangster makes his posthumous lament: Trinidad in all its social tumult is ever present in these stories, but so too are the lives of those with private griefs: a woman mourning the stillbirth of her child; a young mother with cancer facing her mortality. The stories in this collection range wide: across different ethnic communities; across rural and urban settings; across the moneyed elite (and illicit new wealth) and the poor scrabbling for survival; locals and expatriates; the certainties of rational knowledge and the mysteries of the unseen and the uncanny. Different locations in Trinidad are brought to the reader through a precise and sensuous mapping of the country's fauna and flora. Characters thread their way through different stories, but what ties the collection together is Sharon Millar's distinctively personal voice: cool, unsentimental and empathetic. If irony is the only way to inscribe contemporary Trinidad, there is also room for the possibility of redemption.

All titles available from www.peepaltreepress.com